NORTH OF EDEN
AN ANTHOLOGY OF ALASKAN WRITINGS

EDITORS
Brian Hutton, Mark Muro,
Linda Kay Davis, M. Otis Beard.

LOOSE AFFILIATION PRESS
ANCHORAGE, ALASKA

LAYOUT & DESIGN
Tony Sheppard

TECHNICAL ASSISTANCE
T. L. Scott, Rob Lecrone

PUBLISHER
Loose Affiliation
415 D Street #6
Anchorage, Alaska 99501
(907) 278-5826

All rights for the material appearing in this book
are retained by the credited authors.

Copyright LOOSE AFFILIATION © 1995
ISBN 0-9647550-0-9
This project was funded in part by a grant
from the Alaska State Council on the Arts.

PRINTING
A. T. Publishing & Printing, Inc.
Anchorage, Alaska

Contents

Acknowledgements — I
Foreword — IV

Anne Coray
Poetry Workshops — 1
His Sister's Gift
A Source of Strength

Richard Chiappone
Maximum Reception — 4

Marilyn Borell
Dad at 71 — 13

Mike Burwell
Bank of the River — 14

Wayne Mergler
Burial Ground — 16

Mary Kancewick
Village Ascension — 24
Evening Steam

Suzanne Miles
Kenurraq (The Lamp) — 27
(Yup'ik translation by Marie Meade)

John E. Smelcer
Ceremony — 28

Arlitia Jones
Gathering Berries — 29

Linda M. Davis
Baking Bread — 30

Terri D. Doyle
Roselyn Marie and Her New Hair — 34

Brenda Kleinfelder
Winter Air — 39

Karen A. Tschannen
Short Story — 40

Tracy Philpot
    The Infidelity of Birds   41
    The Holiday of Escape

T. L. Scott
    The Bar Maids of Haga Mari   44
    Neighbors

M. Otis Beard
    Amphibian Hand   47
    Inspected By

Ted Herlinger
    Mushrooms   53

Rob Lecrone
    The Headed and the Gutted   58

Krys Holmes
    Eating Alaska   63
    The God That Writes Within Me

Ann Fox Chandonnet
    The Poem is Seeing Things Aloud   69

Marvin Hugo Fuhs
    The Vineyard   70

Robbo
    Just Another Station in Life   71

Monika C. Thomas
    Saline Salvation   73

Tim Young
    Bus Ride   74

Ten Rich
    Toupee   75

Erik Wilson
    TV Mausoleum Dream   76

Contents

Melissa S. Green
  Saturn is Heavier in my Dreams　　77

Mike Firment
  The Day I Got Flowers　　79
    From Georgia O'Keeffe

Nathalie B. Nadeau
  Costa Rica Was Hard on My Shoes　　83

Mark Muro
  Playpen　　87
  Timbuktu

Linda Kay Davis
  Inventory　　91
  Anticipating Emily

Brian Hutton
  Still Life　　93

Francis Broderick
  —the uncertainty principle—　　97

J. Yonug
  Diva's Mailbox　　104

Jeff Byles
  An Interview With the Artist　　109

Contents

Acknowledgements

All acknowledgement pages are perhaps dim shadows of the gratitude felt or the thanks deserved. We find ourselves, for once, at a bit of a loss for the words to adequately express our appreciation of the following friends and supporters:

Terry Sevy and the original members of the writers group for planting the seed of an open forum that has proven to be a vast enrichment for the writers and lovers of the written word in this community and beyond.

Sandy and Jerry Harper and the crew at Cyrano's Bookstore/Café for providing the group with the fertile ground which has allowed it to flourish.

Tracy Hinkson and the folks at Toast Theater for providing Loose Affiliation with non-profit corporation sponsorship for the initial grant proposal.

Tim Wilson and the staff and membership of the Alaska State Council on the Arts for guidance through the grant process which made this project possible.

The Anchorage Press, the Anchorage Daily News, and KRUA radio, for helping us get the word out to the many talented writers we had only suspected were out there.

The 125 writers who submitted over a thousand artifacts of their particular visions, making our lives, for a short while, both a hot, high heaven of heady discovery, and a hell of hard decisions. May the dialogue continue.

Tony Sheppard for the look of the book, endless hours of layout detail and design work, and for pulling together the diverse threads of our imagination into a comprehensible visual whole.

T. L. Scott and Kim Wilson for their humor and behind the scenes critical acuity, in the roles of proofreading wonders and editorial sounding boards.

Rob Lecrone and Duke Russell for a thousand ideas and some very capable hands-on follow through at critical moments.

Nathalie Nadeau and, again, Tony Sheppard, for reminding us that it would be foolish to rush through and not 'do it right' for lack of timely financial support, and for offering said support.

Edith Ewing and Sue Beeman for providing the group with printout capabilities for organizational tasks and crucial missives.

Mike Firment, Catherine Schenk, and countless others, for infinities of support, stability, sanity, and general generosity of spirit.

Whoever it was that left that bag of groceries on my doorstep . . .

Thanks,
Brian Hutton, Mark Muro, Linda Kay Davis,
M. Otis Beard

Foreword

About three years ago I fell in with a small group of writers, largely at the persistence of Terry Sevy, a writer I'd been seeing around for a while in Anchorage coffeehouses, both of us penscratching away at our respective tables, nodding across the room at one another. Occasionally, we found ourselves sitting at the same table, talking between penscratches, sharing little snatches of what we were writing.

For nine months he kept telling me I should drop in on this little writers group, gathering weekly, in various living rooms, gathering steam. I'd been involved in writers groups before, and wasn't particularly in a hurry to 'join' anything.

When I finally took Terry up on his numerous invitations, I was more than favorably impressed. With the quality of the writing. The gentle, yet acute observations offered on the pieces shared within the group. The range of the discussions following. The good and diverse company . . .

More and more people began showing up. It didn't seem to matter much if you were a writer or a friend of a writer, or maybe you were just interested in the things that writers wrote. It was truly a loose affiliation of writers and artists and just generally entertaining people.

The gathering landed eventually in my living room, above Cyrano's Bookstore/Coffee Shop in downtown Anchorage, where it meets even now. We spent our Wednesday evenings for nearly two years, passing pieces back and forth, making comments, and meeting new friends.

We began to notice that some of the work was getting pretty good, and started putting the words out all over Anchorage. At Toast Theater's Crust Festival. On KRUA radio's weekly Local Reader program. In the semi-annual Anchorage Poetry Slam. At the seemingly spontaneously generated art/reading/music Some Thing With Words events.

And we began to show up in various Anchorage publications. Some of them, like the Anchorage Daily News, the Anchorage Press, and The Northern Light and Inklings, of the University of Alaska Anchorage, were already well established. Some, like AK Verve and Quip, came bursting up from out of nowhere in an unprecedented local literary explosion.

Somewhere in there an old friend of mine, Mark Muro, started dropping in on the gatherings, alternately entertaining us and distracting us from the matters at hand with his rapid-fire wit.

I ran into Otis Beard one morning on my way in to tape our weekly radio program, having just missed the bus. The man not only had a car, but a back-log of writings that knocked me over when he read them on the air. He soon became a regular.

Cyrano's let us use their space to begin putting together our own performance venues, like the Get Loose Open Mic Series and the Second Tuesday Solo Series. Mark leading off the Solo Series seemed a natural.

In December of 1994, Mark came charging in with the news that he'd heard Tim Wilson, of the Alaska State Council on the Arts, give a talk on the future of funding for the arts. He described an emerging national trend to fund collaborative literary projects organized by groups with a 'soft hierarchy.' This sounded astoundingly much like what we were up to. We were meeting weekly to discuss our work, pulling together or taking advantage of local group venues, calling ourselves, of all things, Loose Affiliation, and Terry had been making noises lately about us maybe being ready to do an anthology or something. I talked to Tim, who guided us through the grant proposal process, and a month later, the Council granted us some seed money to produce an anthology of Alaskan writing. BOOM!

Suddenly, one Wednesday night we found ourselves looking around the room for volunteers to act as editors for this awesome undertaking. Otis said, "Absolutely!" Mark said, "Sure." I said, "Well, okay," as Terry had unfortunately just left us to spend some time with family in Portland.

None of the three of us had ever had any experience with editing before, so we had our naiveté working for us, at any rate, but we all three wrote and read and we knew some damned good writers. So we were off and running, coming up with imaginary schedules and deadlines, putting the word out, researching the printing process, trying to figure out if we knew somebody who knew somebody who knew something about . . . .

And just about the time when the first writings started to trickle in, before the check in the mail had arrived, Mark had to take a trip to New York. So it was Otis and I, reading like crazy, running around like crazy, making tough decisions about whether to buy a pack of smokes or make more copies of the Call for Submissions flyer and somehow managing both.

The Anchorage Press invited us to coordinate a creative writing section, which was too good to pass on, though we were struggling to keep the venues that we had rolling. The trickle had become a torrent. The rent was due. And overdue. We were out of smokes. It was cold outside. In wandered Linda Kay Davis with editing experience, some killer poetry, a great of sense of the absurd and extra smokes, and she agreed to be our fourth editor. Whew!

By the time Mark returned from New York, we'd begun to find some of the most incredible pieces of writing in our mailbox. More writers than we'd realized were out there. More diversity than we'd even imagined. We heard from writers whose work you will see here in print for the very first time. Writers who have been published in various prestigious literary journals across the nation.

We'd decided early on that the focus of the book would not be merely stories about the 'Alaskan experience.' That had been done. And it was not particularly what the writers in our group were writing about. We were interested in showing off some of the range of writings by Alaskan writers.

However, there was a quality in some of the pieces about Alaska that could not be ignored. There were also edgy urban pieces. Subtle pieces about life and death and relationships. Quirky, funny pieces about sex and writing and other passions. We are more convinced than ever that contemporary writing in Alaska is nothing if it is not diverse. We think we've been moderately successful in displaying some of this diversity. We think you'll enjoy it.

Oddly enough, we kept meeting new friends along the way . . .

Brian Hutton

Anne Coray

POETRY WORKSHOPS

Sometimes, you want to take out
your midnight .22—
blast through the starched
white frock of logic,
splash a little blood
on his bleached cuffs.

Your thermos is full of hot spit.
You wish you had the guts
to share it.

You'd like to clot the air
with dark words and smells—
voodoos and witches' chants,
rank or rotting flesh.

Sometimes, you consider uncloseting
your pneumatic jack-hammer,
fracturing linoleum and cement
in a six-foot diameter
in the room's center.

You long to uncover
earth, fire, stones, burials,
the corpse of Neruda.

Sometimes, you know you have known
for a long, long time
this other depth
and how it is
you keep committing suicide.

Anne Coray

HIS SISTER'S GIFT

On Christmas morning, the child
wakes, anticipation piled
up like clothing on the floor.
He dresses, runs unbridled

down the stairs to the closed door
of his parents' room. He's sure
they're awake, but he softly
peeks in. His drumming heart's core

stiffens. He backsteps slowly
down the hall to the false tree,
opens his sister's gift, rubs
the rigid breasts of Barbie.

Anne Coray

A SOURCE OF STRENGTH

The river spreads her fat-fisted uterus
Before the sand spit's tongue.
Glacial hounds ripped and tore
Raw her breasts. Now she rests
With an old longing,
A dull knife's edge.

What she has left for fingers
Are chopped knuckles;
An Indian woman's grieving
Echoes like vast bells.

This is a country without metrics
Whose wells suck up rhyme.
Submerge me.
Wrap your entrails of cold clay
About my face.
Spline my limp body
With your stiff trees.

Richard Chiappone

MAXIMUM RECEPTION

The morning after his retirement party, Delton went out and bought the satellite dish. He paid cash, made arrangements for its delivery, returned home, and sliced a six-foot-square patch out of his front lawn where he thought it should sit. All morning, he worked on the hole for the pad, rolling up the sod and hauling it to the curb, fighting the root-webs and nested glacial rocks as he dug deeper. It was a warm June day, the solstice sun high over the Chugach Mountains, east of Anchorage, and Delton was sweating fiercely when Fay came down from the house and stood by the gaping excavation.

He'd told her he wanted the dish, but he hadn't made it clear how much concrete would be needed to support it. He watched her survey their otherwise tidy yard: the lush iris beds, the peonies, the big weeping birch with its willowy branches sweeping right down to their fine lawn. She paused a moment and took in the little mountain ash she had planted the autumn before, smiling—Delton supposed—at the memory of it festooned with bars of perfumed soap to ward off browsing moose. She stared at the exposed dirt, the ends of worms, then directly at Delton.

"You think it's going to be that much better than cable, Del?"

"We've got to stay in touch, Fay," he said. He leaned against the handle of the shovel and mopped his brow with his hanky.

Fay looked at him closely.

"You'll get used to this, Del. It's going to be all right—really."

Delton knew she meant to be reassuring, but there was something in her voice that sounded a lot like pity.

The satellite dish was the biggest residential model the store sold. Delton had asked about the units for hotels and apartment houses, but the salesman assured him the one he'd bought "would bring in everything that was out there."

"I guess you'll be needing an installer?" the man said. He

produced a business card from the breast pocket of his sport coat.

Delton had worked on dams, pipelines, every kind of road and bridge in Alaska, but this was a little technical, electronic. He took the card:

> J. RONNIE COOVER
> Communications Advisor
> Anchorage. Fairbanks. Juneau.

There were three phone numbers.

When he tried the local number, a message machine said the call had been forwarded to Fairbanks, that Coover would be checking in by remote. Delton was impressed. J. Ronnie Coover was clearly a man comfortable with technology. Delton left a message and spent the rest of the day working on the hole in his front lawn.

Just before supper, a delivery truck pulled up. Two young men with ponytails and muscles like melons wrestled the big steel halves of the satellite dish off the truck and onto the grass. Delton hustled to off-load the smaller boxes and coils of wire. Then he fetched three beers. He and the boys stood in the driveway and drank, swatting the mosquitoes.

"It's a big one, isn't it?" Delton said over the rim of his beer can.

"Heavy fucker," one boy said. He set a sneakered foot on the edge of the dish.

The other boy looked at the pit Delton had dug. "Installing it yourself?"

Delton smiled. "Mostly."

It was the best he'd felt since his retirement party.

As they cleared the dinner table, Fay said, "You're pushing yourself a bit, aren't you, Del?"

He knew where she was heading. She was going to want to talk about it, about him and what was on his mind. It was her way, and he didn't really mind it in small doses. He liked it, in fact. But, if he was going to be home all day, every day, now, well...

"I'd like to get the concrete poured in case this guy Coover can wire the dish right away. That's all," Delton said.

"Is that why you've been out there all day?"

"Fay, I'm doing fine."

"I heard more from you when you worked out in the bush."

Delton pushed back from the table. He didn't want this to turn into anything more than it had to.

"We'll talk about this later, O.K.? I have a couple of things I want to get done yet."

He went outside and worked into the evening, taking advantage of the lingering sun, cutting the hole deeper and deeper, making room for the pea gravel and concrete that would support the dish. It was 11:30 when Fay called him from the porch—J. Ronnie Coover was on the phone from Fairbanks.

"Caught me between jobs," Coover said in a high, metallic voice. "I'll be down straight away to pick the spot. Don't pour the pad yet."

"But I got a place all cleared."

"It's got to be right. That satellite is in a stationary orbit up there. It's geosynchronous. Either you're aiming at it or you're not."

Delton shifted the receiver to his other ear. He looked out the window at the big hole in the middle of his front yard. He already had the bags of concrete mix stacked next to it, the hose, the wheelbarrow to mix it in. He wondered again if he could figure out the electronics by himself. A bulldozer, yes. A grader, a steamroller, no sweat. But he could barely operate the microwave. The VCR mystified him. *Geosynchronous?*

"You still with me?" Coover shrilled.

"I only got so much yard."

"I'll be right down," Coover said. "Next flight, for sure."

Delton hung up the phone.

"Another hole?" Fay said.

He sank into his big chair in front of the TV, clicked the set on, and grazed through the channels. Then he turned it off again. "This guy's the best there is, Fay. Coming all the way down from Fairbanks. If he says we have to dig a bit more..."

Fay stood at the screen door, glumly looking out at the wrecked yard.

"This is all new to me," Delton said. "I'm trying to get used to it."

"Me too," Fay said. "It's new to me too. Come on. Let's get

some sleep. I don't imagine our Mr. Coover will be here before morning."

"You go on ahead," he said. "I'll be right up."

He wandered outside to look at the dish one more time. He stepped down into the big hole he had dug, pressed his hands flat against his lower back, and peered up at the pink evening sky until it made him dizzy wondering about that stationary orbit. How could anything hang there in one spot without moving and without falling back to earth? The idea made his head hurt.

Out in the bog behind the house, wood frogs struck up a disjointed squawking. He listened to their ragged song for a moment, then limped back inside. He set the alarm carefully for seven, and crawled into bed next to Fay.

Delton woke to the sound of a car door slamming in front of the house. He sat up, confused. The daylight coming through the curtains seemed to be the same intensity as it had been when he'd gotten in bed, though the clock on the night stand read 2:25. Someone outside was shouting in a high, tinny voice. Delton got to the window in time to see an orange taxi swerve away from the curb. There was a man standing in his driveway. Fay was snoring softly. Delton grabbed his pants and ran downstairs.

J. Ronnie Coover was rooting through one of the half-dozen big steel toolboxes, battered and plastered with airline stickers, that lay at his feet. He was young—in his early twenties maybe—and had a wispy, first-growth beard. One ear lobe was crammed with fine gold loops and what appeared to be a fishing lure, but Delton had been on construction long enough to know that wild looks meant nothing when the work started.

Coover smiled up at Delton and continued poking through his tools until he came up with a compass and something that looked like a sextant. He stood and offered his free hand.

"Caught the last flight of the night," he said, once again startling Delton with the strained pitch of his voice. "I love dish jobs."

"You want to put your stuff inside until morning?"

Coover looked up at the sky. The sun was already showing above the mountains.

"It *is* morning."

He took off across the front lawn at a brisk pace, walked right by the big pit Delton had dug, and stopped closer to the house. He looked up again, held the instrument to his eye, and jotted something in his notebook. He laid the ends of a tape measure on the grass and extended it a yard or two until it was nearly touching Fay's mountain ash.

"Here we go," he said. "Give me a hand."

Using four wooden stakes and some heavy white cord, they roped off the new location for the concrete slab. The ash was just inside the corner of the square.

"We get that little tree out of the way, we got it knocked," Coover said, his voice cutting through the neighborhood like a siren. "Maximum reception!"

Fay had planted the mountain ash for the Bohemian waxwings its berries attracted. Birding was one of the things she suggested they take up when Delton retired. "Let's make a list," she'd said, "for our new life." She wrote Travel, Bird Watching, Gardening. Delton poked at his sheet of paper for a few minutes, his mind a desert, then copied Fay's.

Delton and Coover worked until six a.m., assembling the two halves of the dish on the lawn. Then, when it was clear that there was nothing more they could do until the tree was moved and a new hole dug for the concrete pad, Delton talked Coover into taking a break. Coover pulled a tiny Japanese TV out of his toolbox and plugged it into the outlet on Delton's porch. They sat watching the news and talking quietly. Delton was pleased to hear that Coover had been on some big jobs—the Performing Arts Center, the museum downtown. Like Delton, Coover had worked out in the bush, too, in the native villages, the mining and lumber towns. They traded stories about miserable superintendents, know-nothing architects. Around seven, they heard Fay in the kitchen fixing breakfast.

Delton tried to work up a smile as he broke the news about her tree.

"Move it? In mid-summer? Its roots are working full-time," Fay said.

Delton mumbled something about reception.

Fay turned to Coover.

"What's wrong with the roof?"

"Dish is way too big. First wind'll rip out the trusses. Saw it happen in Juneau."

"The back yard?"

"House will block nearly everything."

Fay pinched the bridge of her nose. She leaned back against the counter.

Delton examined his napkin. Coover stirred in his chair. "Got to make a call," he said. He walked out of the room, punching numbers into the cellular phone he wore on his belt.

"Look, Del," Fay said quietly, "he seems like a nice enough boy and all, but he shows up here in the middle of the night and wants to cut my tree down."

"To *move* it," Delton said. "We need to move it a bit."

Fay brushed that aside: "You already dug a hole the size of a grave out there. I'm trying to be reasonable. Is this what it's going to be like from now on?"

Delton heard Coover go out the front door.

"I don't know, Fay," he said. "These things are complicated. They're complex."

"What's it going to be next week, Del, and the week after that? A tunnel? Pyramids?"

Delton got up from the table. "I'll talk to Coover," he said. He headed for the door.

"Coover?" Fay said. "It's not Coover that needs talking to."

Delton joined Coover on the lawn. They stood looking at the tree, but his mind was on Fay. Maybe he *was* moving a little fast.

"This is coming between you two," Coover said. "I'll step aside for a while, go see a friend here in town, get some sleep maybe. I'll call you later."

"You could sleep here," Delton said.

"Here's my cab now."

Coover started down the driveway, waving at the approaching taxi. He ran around to the passenger side.

"You talk it over with the missus. Let me know what you

want to do." He paused, leaning across the roof of the cab. "Could auger a hole, drop a pole in it, some concrete, mount that big sucker up on top, maybe." He shrugged. "Might work."

Delton turned and looked at the dish. He tried to visualize it up on a pole, high above the yard. When he turned back, Coover was gone.

It was close to noon when Delton pulled back into the driveway. Strapped to the door handles of his old Cadillac was a black steel pipe that extended out beyond both the front and rear fenders. Small red flags flapped at each end.

Fay watched silently as Delton untied one end of the big pipe and lowered it to the driveway. He cut the other end loose and let it fall with a fierce clamor, then hustled around to the trunk, and hauled a heavy gas-powered auger out and set it next to the pipe.

"What in God's name?" Fay said.

Delton's hip ached, his back ached, his shoulders throbbed, but he couldn't stop smiling. He leaned close to Fay and whispered, "The beauty is the tree won't have to move."

Fay looked at the long spiral blade of the auger. "Not even going to ask," she said. She turned and walked toward the house. "I'll fix some lunch."

When she came back out to tell him the food was ready, she found a cloud of oily, blue exhaust hanging over the yard. In the middle of it, Delton stood drilling a hole in the lawn a few feet from the mountain ash. She watched the black soil curl off the auger bit as it corkscrewed into the earth. Delton could see that she fully expected the little tree to disappear as its roots became entangled in the machine.

When he backed the auger out, he had a neat round hole.

"Perfect, isn't it?" he said. "The dish'll clear the tree by ten feet, and it'll be years before the branches even reach it. Then we can just sort of prune around it, you see?" Delton glanced at his watch. "I just wish Coover would call."

Suddenly a yawn came over him that he couldn't stifle, and Fay took him by the arm. "Come on, buster," she said. "You didn't sleep at all last night. Lunch, then it's nap time." She led him back up to the house.

He walked along in a daze. A nap? To the best of his knowledge, he hadn't taken a nap since he was five years old. Why didn't she just embalm him?

"I don't think I can sleep," he said. "I really don't."

All afternoon, Delton paced from the yard to the house and back again, convinced that there was something he could be doing while he waited for Coover to call. He tried sitting by the phone, but only lasted a few minutes before going out to look at the newly augered hole once more.

Fay was asleep on the couch, her needlework on the floor nearby. In the window above her, the afternoon sky had turned a sour gray. Rain was beginning to streak the glass at a sharp, wind-driven angle. The house felt cold.

Delton covered Fay with an afghan and stood looking at her. She looked so stiff and still, her mouth slightly open. She could sleep, he thought. He wondered if he'd ever want to again. He looked around the room, trying to remember the last time he had a whole afternoon with absolutely nothing to do. He wandered out to the front yard.

The neighborhood was quiet. A trace of rain glistened on the empty street. A gust of wind tore at the mountain ash, twisting its leaves to expose their silvery undersides. A corner of the tarp he had placed over the concrete sacks flapped furiously, and he walked down and put a rock on it.

The rain began in earnest then, and it felt good. It felt like a thousand cold wet mornings on job sites from the Aleutians to the North Slope. He could smell diesel and the hot asphalt of a new road. He could smell sawdust and plywood, and oiled concrete forms, and he felt rejuvenated.

He pulled back the tarp and heaved a sack of concrete mix up into the wheelbarrow, ripped it open, ran the garden hose into it, and stirred it with the shovel. When it looked right, he poured the mix down into the augered hole. Then he went for the pipe.

But the pipe was too long, too awkward, and way too heavy for one man, young or old, to carry. He had to straddle the pipe, drag it to the hole, walking backwards. Pain shot from his neck to the soles of his feet. He felt the lack of sleep suddenly, as a fluttering in his eyelids.

Positioning one end of the pipe at the rim of the hole, he hurried to the other end and hefted it to his knees. Then he jerked it to chest level and pinned it there as it snagged on the lip of the hole and stalled. He heaved it up to his shoulder, but it could go no further.

The rain became a downpour, carried on gusts that bent the ash almost to the ground. Dense drops lashed his face. He felt his feet sliding on the wet grass, the pipe slipping through his palms.

The dead weight of it—at first a matter for his back and legs—was now beginning to tell as a quivering in his chest and shoulders. He felt his pulse throbbing in the big artery in his neck where it pressed against the pipe. His ears began to ring. Spots circled at the backs of his eyes.

He found himself thinking about all the projects he'd been on over the years, how they hadn't seemed like anything but tasks to complete at the time, but how they now looked like pieces of a life. He cut a glance at the satellite dish lying on the lawn, the tools and supplies all around him. He wanted badly to finish this job, but the pipe was driving him to the ground.

Then the wood frogs started up, the racket growing as though the satellite dish had already begun funneling and focusing the sounds of Delton's new life.

There was something else, too. A blooming, color-flooded vision forming. Delton squinted at the strain. He felt something give, a welling-up in his chest. He closed his eyes to the flowering pain and saw Fay leaning out over the porch railing. She was wearing a yellow dress, tight and shapely over her hips. Her hair was dark, and long, free and blowing in the wind. It was the way she'd worn it when she was young. Her lips seemed as red as the mountain-ash berries.

She called out, "Delton."

It came to him, over the wind, the rain, and the frogs—maximum reception—and he pushed once more, the pipe as weightless now as time itself.

sat with Lutie the second night. After that, because the weather was getting hot that time of year, the business of burial had to be quickly undertaken.

"I want Aunt Lutie buried at the Old Place," Grandmother had tearfully declared one night at supper. "With her people. She spent all but the last twenty-three years of her life there. She belongs there."

"Must I remind you, woman, that the Old Place no longer belongs to our family?" Grandfather said. He was upset. Just mention of the Old Place always upset him, Perry knew.

"I don't care," Grandmother replied. "The people who live there now just be decent Christian people. If so, they'll let us bury Lutie in the old slave graveyard there."

Grandmother would have her way. Father made the arrangements to transport the body in Jake's coffin on the train. He and Grandfather and Great-aunt Susan would accompany Grandmother on the journey. It was decided at the last minute, by Grandfather, that Perry would go, too.

"The boy should see the Old Place, should know where he comes from," he said. "And what he's lost."

The night before they left, Grandmother found Perry seated on the porch steps watching the lightning bugs glimmer and flicker against the black of night.

"You have to pay your respects to the dead, child. You haven't yet. Come say good-bye to poor old Aunt Lutie."

She imprisoned him in her big, fleshy arms. Grandmother was a big, plain-faced woman, raw-boned and heavy, with gray hair and ruddy, work-roughened skin, but she was loving and good, and Perry submitted to her will despite his sinking fear of the corpse locked behind the library doors and allowed himself to be drawn toward the coffin Jake had made. There the tiny withered crone lay like a corn-cob doll among the satiny interior.

"Look at her, love," Grandmother crooned. Perry tried to hold back, but Grandmother pulled him closer. "She can't hurt you, honey. She's dead."

But those were the very words that struck terror in the child's heart. That night, in the dark nursery, he huddled beneath his blankets, trembling, certain that old black Lutie was creeping, like a spidery, whispering shadow, up the hall stairs to get him.

"Come here to Lutie, sweet baby," the whisper swept along the papered walls of the hall. "Come see me one las' time, honey."

He heard those haunting whispers until, at last, he fell into a troubled, fitful sleep.

They took the Danville train the next day—Father, Grandfather, Grandmother, Great-aunt Susan, and Perry. Jake drove them to the railway station in the buggy, while his sons Ludus and Kester followed in the buckboard with the coffin. It was the first trip in the cars for Perry and he sat, all eyes, by the window. He was seated next to Grandfather who looked so distinguished in his Sunday suit with his long white beard combed out like a frothy bib down his ample front and his best straw hat on his head. Perry thought that Father, in his plain dark suit, and Grandmother and Great-aunt Susan, in their black dresses and wide hats, seemed dull and drab in Grandfather's company.

Perry watched the foothills of the Blue Ridge countryside roll by. They clattered through farmland which looked much like the scenery in and around Lynchburg, but to the little boy at the window it was all new and wonderful. Once they passed a little black boy sitting on a fence by the railroad tracks who reminded him of Kester. The little black boy grinned and waved, and Perry, delighted, returned the wave. They waved eagerly and happily to each other, like old comrades, until the boy on the fence vanished at last behind a bend of trees.

Perry sat back, suddenly lonely.

"Perry, do you understand where we are going?" Grandfather asked him.

"To put Aunt Lutie in the ground," the child replied.

"Yes, but do you know where?"

"The Old Place," said Perry.

"Do you know what the Old Place is?" Grandfather persisted.

"No, sir," Perry admitted. He felt slightly ashamed of himself. He sensed that he was supposed to know about the Old Place.

Marilyn Borell

DAD AT 71

You slipped into December's
window of light
on borrowed skis, breaking snow
like dinner plates.
Poles too tall, you gripped midnight
blue shanks, propelled yourself along.

You'd spoken of Wisconsin
winters, your wild
flights down Henderson's Hill
on barrel staves.
Fretting over brittle bones,
I nearly missed the boy beneath the grey.

Mike Burwell

BANK OF THE RIVER

A lively understandable spirit
Once entertained you.
It will come again.
      Theodore Roethke

The river's slicing
tells us the way back
upstream
to the genesis of light
when words trembled down
from primitive branches
leaped from inchoate birds
rose out of root and soft soil,
a place where long
distillations of light
and weather made voices.

They talk more swiftly than bones,
have no greater power
than their own appearance
waiting for the listener
who can hear the ashes
beneath words.

At night
the voice of the steep bank
gets up to inhabit the air,
walks around in rocks,
sleeps in the skin of caribou,
visits other banks:
its own kind.

Voices join, stride
together over water,
slide chattering downstream
to lodge in our dreaming.

From our boats
we see these banks as
merely beautiful
but often remember
a gliding in our sleep:
the sacrifice of the unseen.

Wayne Mergler

BURIAL GROUND

Old Aunt Lutie died when Perry was six. She had been ill, even dying, all his life. The ancient black woman, the former slave who had reared Grandmother Wheeler from infancy, was the oldest person Perry had ever seen. Rarely did she leave her tiny attic room, but sometimes Jake carried her down the long flights of stairs so that she could sit, on a hot summer's evening, on the porch and talk with the family. It was on Perry that most of the old woman's attention was fixed. She would hold out her claw-like brown hands to him and whisper hoarsely: "Come see old Aunt Lutie, you sweet thing." No one knew Lutie's age, not even Lutie herself, but Grandmother said she was near a hundred is she was a day, and Perry believed it. She was emaciated to the point of feebleness, as dry as a wisp of winter straw, with brown skin fantastically wrinkled and thin, wispy white hair clinging to a nut-like head. Perry cowered from her when she beckoned him and clutched at Mother or Grandmother, until poor old Lutie would say, in her hoarse dry whisper: "Bless your heart, you sweet baby, I know I'm so old and ugly."

She died quietly in her bed one night in the early spring, and Grandmother, as grief-stricken as if Aunt Lutie had been a blood relation, insisted that the body be laid out in the library. Jake made the coffin with his own big, black hands in a makeshift workshop in the stable. He cut the boards himself, hammered and sawed, sandpapered, and fitted pieces together, while Perry and Jake's boy Kester silently watched. Grandmother gave Jake an old satin comforter to use for the coffin's lining. When it was finished Jake himself carried down the body that Grandmother and Jake's wife Anselma had washed and dressed in one of Grandmother's gowns and placed in the coffin in the library. Grandmother sat up with the body that first night. In his upstairs room, with the door open, Perry could hear the steady creaking of her rocking chair in the silence of the house. Great-aunt Susan

"The Old Place," Grandfather explained," is your ancestral home, boy. Your father was born there, as was your grandmother before him."

"Were you born there too, Grandfather?"

"No. I married into the place, but I can tell you, boy, I loved that place far more than anyone who *was* born there. I farmed that land, I raised cattle there and some of the finest horses ever seen in the Piedmont. I raised five boys there, too, and then buried four of 'em in the war. Only your father is left. Do you understand all this, son?"

"I—think so." Perry was hesitant.

"Then we lost it all," Grandfather went on. "They took it away from us." Perry saw that the old man's big, brown-spotted hands had begun to tremble as they rested on his knees.

"Who took it from us, Grandfather?"

"Who? Who, indeed, boy? I'll tell you who. It was the Yankees and the niggers, that's who. And I hope to God you never forget it!"

"Ethan," said Grandmother softly.

"Well, it's the truth, woman, and you know it. The boy needs to be told the truth."

"Lutie is a nigger," Perry said, simply.

A sharp silence fell like an ax. Only the clacketing noise of the fast-moving train could be heard.

They left the train at the little village of Altavista, some twenty miles short of Danville. There Father hired two Negroes with shovels and rented two hitched buckboards. They drove down the hilly, red-clay track west to the Old Place. It was a pretty drive now in spring, for the cherry and apple trees were in blossom and limbs hung with the fragrant white flowers arched over the red clay road as they passed in the wagons beneath. Ahead, the Blue Ridge lay smoky and blue as its name in the distance. One of the hired Negroes drove the second wagon with Grandfather seated next to him on the seat and the other Negro in the back with the shovels and pick-axes. Father drove the first wagon. Seated at his side were Grandmother and Great-aunt Susan. Perry had to sit in the back of the first wagon with the coffin. The muddy country rut was rough and bumpy, and with every bounce the coffin slid across the floorboards of the wagon bed, scraping with a groaning noise which agitated his nerves. He feared that the coffin lid would fly open and Lutie herself would come bouncing out to cling to him with her skeletal brown hands. They rode in that hot sun for nearly two hours, breathing dust and bogging down in red clay mires, before they came at last to meadows of rolling green hills where cattle grazed in lazy indifference to the wagons coming up the road. And there, just beyond the fields, with the Blue Ridge hazy as wood smoke in its backyard, stood a stately white house.

"There it is," Grandmother said, and even six-year-old Perry could recognize the emotion in her voice.

Perry saw the splendid white house and the apple and cherry orchards and the great walnut trees spreading out like they owned the whole place. There was a big, unpainted barn he saw and smaller outbuildings—a smokehouse, a springhouse, maybe even a blacksmithy.

"That's the house your daddy was born in, and all his poor dead brothers, too," Grandmother said. She pulled a handkerchief from her sleeve and wiped at her eyes.

For a while the house wove in and out of view as the road twisted and turned through trees and tangled shrubbery. They passed an unpainted frame house at the side of the road, dilapidated and abandoned now, its windows broken, its front door hanging limp on its hinges.

"That's where our overseer lived," Grandmother said. "But he's been gone since before the war."

They emerged from the trees once more and the fields stretched out around them. The house was closer now. A young horse, seeing the wagons coming, galloped along the split-rail fence as if thrilled by the sight of them. Father turned onto the lane which led to the house and drove to its end, pulling up under a spreading walnut tree. Grandfather's wagon came up beside them.

A white woman in a sunbonnet emerged from the garden through a gate in the split-rail fence. She carried a basket of early squash. She was a heavy, red-faced woman, and she stopped when she saw the strangers and waited for them to explain themselves. Grandfather stepped down from the wagon and walked towards her. Perry noticed once again how fine and gentlemanly he looked in his Sunday suit and how he tipped his straw hat to the work-worn woman. Perry could not hear all that was said, but he caught words "old slave woman" and "slave burying ground." He saw the sunbonneted woman nodding her head, saw her glance toward the group in the wagons once or twice. In a moment a man came out of the house and joined Grandfather and the woman. An old Negro man came from the barn and stood looking curiously on at the newcomers.

"Lord," Grandmother murmured from her seat on the wagon. "I don't see a single face I know."

Perry heard the white man talking to Grandfather say: "Your wife's old mammy?" And Grandfather nodded.

Apparently permission was granted, for Grandfather came back to the buckboard, climbed in, and said, "Let's go." Even Perry knew that it galled his grandfather to have to ask permission to use the land he still thought of as rightfully his own. The wagon bounced over the grassy pasture land beyond the barn, down the gently bucking landscape until it came to a halt by a grove of cedar trees.

"Where's the graveyard?" Perry asked.

"Right here," Grandmother said. She waved vaguely toward a field of tall grasses and tangled weeds at the edge of the cedar grove.

"But—where are the gravestones?" the child pursued.

"No gravestones in a slave graveyard," said Grandmother.

"Then how do you know whose grave it whose?"

"You remember, if you can," she answered.

The two Negroes hired in Altavista began to dig at once beneath a tall cedar tree.

"Oh, Lutie'd like that," Grandmother said. "She always liked to sit in the shade."

The little party stood quietly by as the men dug the grave. Perry looked into the hole. The damp, loamy smell of red Virginia clay rose up from the deep coolness. He shuddered and drew back. To think that old black Lutie in her coffin would sleep there forever! When the grave was dug, Father and Grandfather helped the men lower the coffin into the red clay. Grandmother and Great-aunt Susan stood together beneath Lutie's tree, a curious pair—tall, raw-boned Grandmother, short, dumpy Susan. Perry watched the red earth shoveled onto the coffin, heard it land with dull thudding noises against the wood. Gradually the sound grew softer and the damp hole closed forever over old Lutie. She could not get to him now. The earth was as solid over her as if it had swallowed her up.

When it was over and the others had returned to the wagons, Grandfather took Perry by the hand and together they stood looking over the panorama of the farm that for so many years had been their family home site. Fertile pastures and dense forests flowed out unspoiled clear to the river.

"Perry," the old man spoke at last. "Look around you good and remember all this. This is the most important thing there is. Land. Earth, fields, and trees. See those woods yonder, boy? They are alive with life. Right here by this burying place is more life than you can imagine. There are deer in there and foxes, jackrabbits, coyotes, bobcats. Bald eagles fly over them trees, boy. Some of them trees are so full of passenger pigeons that the branches are broken beneath 'em and the ground is sticky and white from their droppings. Get you some land like this someday, boy, and work it and love it and don't ever let nobody take it from you. This land would've been yours someday, boy, but the war robbed you of it." The old familiar bitterness crept into his grandfather's voice. "Don't you ever forget, boy, what the damn Yankees and the niggers took away from you."

Perry did not understand what the Negroes had to do with it. As far as he could see the Negroes were only buried under these tall weeds with no gravestones to even mark where they lay. What had they taken from him? Lutie as a Negro and here Grandfather had come all this way just to bury her under a cedar tree where she would feel at home. It was all a mystery to him, but he knew not to ask about this.

In the wagon Grandmother said: "Honey, come sit on my lap. I need some hugs." Perry scrambled onto the wagon seat between Father and Great-aunt Susan and sank into the voluminous folds of his grandmother's skirts, which smelled vaguely of pine trees and old lavender water and dust.

"You know, old Lutie was more of a mamma to me than my own mamma was," Grandmother told him, as the wagon began to move along. "My mamma died when I wasn't but two years old. Lutie took me over. She wasn't very young even then—over forty, I'd say. But she was strong and wiry and brown, and she had a laugh that could be heard clear to Altavista when something tickled her. I loved that old nigger woman." She blew her nose on her damp, soiled handkerchief. "She always used to say to me when I was a little gal no bigger'n you that when we died, like my mamma had died, it wasn't really a thing to be sad about because we went back to the earth. Our bodies, she said, soon become part of the trees and the grass and the flowers—and our souls, well, they become birds, Lutie said. 'Lawd, I'd like to be a bird,' Lutie said."

The sun was low in the sky over the smoky blue Ridge as the two wagons rolled over the bumpy farmland and on to the red clay track that would take them back to town. As they passed through the apple and cherry orchards, so dazzling now with the setting sun pinkening their clustered blossoms, a great flapping noise rose up from the woods behind them. Perry turned to see an enormous flock of passenger pigeons surge up into the sky, temporarily obliterating the sun, like an eclipse, as they swept along toward the hazy mountains in the distance.

"Oh, look!" Perry cried.

Never had he seen so many birds. Darkness fell over the land like night as the birds flew. The sound of their wings was like the cracking of thunder and Perry could feel the wind from their flight as if a storm was brewing.

"Lutie's there," Grandmother whispered into his ear.

Only gradually did the sun begin to return, reappearing in isolated bright bits between the flapping wings of the pigeons.

"Good-bye, Lutie," Perry whispered, as the last pigeon raced across the sun. "I wish I had let you hug me."

Slowly, in the setting sun, the two wagons rolled on down the road to where the train would be waiting.

Mary Kancewick

VILLAGE ASCENSION

a response to "Bypassing Rue Descartes"
by Czeslaw Milocz

I ascend from the river, shy, an intruder,
a white person just come to a Native village.

Ashamed to remember the habits of my house
I accept food from strangers, wipe my plate clean.
Keep quiet. Keep counsel. Keep trying

to understand what is being misunderstood.
I enter the woods blinded by the shade and frightened.

What options, ways, present themselves? Cut down
the trees? Climb one into sun? Or wait for my eyes
to adjust to given light?

Meanwhile the village behaves in accordance with its
    nature,
sleeping and waking all hours in the all-hour light,
checking nets set for salmon in beargun-weighted boats,
cleaning, cutting, drying fish gathered like manna—
indifferent to progress, productivity, rising GNPs,

all tended by others in other countries
with different religions and different heavens,
different songs, dances, and things called serpents.

I look away, lean against birch, less than hum.
Think, rocks everywhere are so old you have to kiss
    them.

Mary Kancewick

EVENING STEAM

There come to me the voices
of Yupik women in the steamy dark.
There they bead their skin
with a water born of fire—
with beads that pull into threads,
stitching over skin like lace,
into veils that net and knot,
place and pull from place:
a sharpness, a dissolve.

Outside, children's voices
drop into the night, like
bits of ice, shattering, musically,
onto the road, from house eves.
Someone names each child.
On my lips, my tongue tastes salt.

A basin is passed, a cloth, a dipper,
a bucket of cool water.
From the melding of molecules,
we reclaim our momentary skins.

Suzanne Miles

KENURRAQ
(The Lamp)

<u>Arnaq kenurrailnguq caituq</u> . . .
strong as whalebone, these old words—
"A woman without a lamp has nothing."

A small ivory boat, ancient, stained
cracked and veined with carrying light,
worn smooth in passing from palm to palm—

Feel the breath of the last
woman to light its wick,
knowing within that steady glow
everything she saw, her own.

(Yup'ik translation, Marie Meade)

John E. Smelcer

CEREMONY

for Kenny B.

I bury a pine seed in a shallow field where trees are born
and turn my face up to the patient sky.

Along this river edge, so long ago, roasting salmon
on thin willows cut green from a cool shroud of forest shadow,
we could not know then as boys
how you would waste your resistance
in the quiet company of strangers and dissolution,
until it faded like your jeans and you would raise a rusted barrel
to end the fragrant memories of youth.

In the gray shade of dusk I see the black bird of your spirit
rising like a feather above the ancient river and narrow field
into a dark and rolling sundown slowly stealing
towards the blue light of a distant pink mountain.

Arlitia Jones

GATHERING BERRIES

Crouched low to quilted tundra
she gathers cranberries that roll
like rosary beads between her fingers

and fall against the tin-bright bottom
of an old can like one-word prayers
spoken soft against a child's skin.

Her back tires. She straightens
and thinks of her grandson
born with a crooked spine, stunted

like the trunk of a black spruce,
brittle with its own growth and hung
with chimes of dried branches in wind.

She presses her hands to the broad plane
that is the small of her back and hopes
he will learn to grow low to the ground.

The berries glint, with them she will put away
a compote for his first birthday.
She bends to a tapestry of moss and leaves.

don't, don't, say the berries as she drops
them, one by one. *He is too young,* says the can
growing heavy in the crook of her arm.

Linda M. Davis

BAKING BREAD

I feel the texture and moisture level of the dough change as I work it. The palms of my hands, held together at the base of the mound, push down, then fingers curl around the bulge that surges forward under the pressure of my palms. A quick flip from eight fingers rotates the mound one-quarter turn to the right while the wrists stay poised for the next thrust downward. The dough sticks to the counter, and I sprinkle flour on it and the counter, and rub the little bits that are stuck to the smooth surface into little mounds and push them way down into the center of the ball.

I stand to the right of the kitchen window that looks out onto one-third acre of head-high native grasses mixed with wild rose and raspberry bushes. The field is surrounded to the sides and behind the house by alders and 75-foot white spruce. In front of the house beyond the field and my gardens is the Stony River. Up river 35 miles is Lime Village, population 42, and down river 35 miles is Stony River Village, with about he same. Above the river and the tops of the willows and cottonwoods on the other side, I see the Lime Hills and the mountain where the Sparrevohn Air Force site lies about 50 miles across the tundra. At night I can see a light there from my upstairs bedroom window.

Occasionally, I look out the window at the sunshine as my hands work the dough. I rock slightly backward and forward with the motions that repeat until the surface skin of the dough starts to break.

This is usually a private time for me, time to allow my mind to wander and imagine. I imagine my fingers are poised above a keyboard and I am a great pianist playing "Prelude in C Flat Minor," like my mother used to, with vigor and drama. Or I imagine the mound is ocean water that surges in waves as it gushes from under my palms, then recedes for the next wave, as I rhythmically sway.

But right now, my partner sits behind me to my left, 15 feet across the room at the kitchen table. He is upset. At least he appears to be. He tells me about a behavior of mine that bugs him, and I consider it. "Yes," I say, "I see your point. That would bother me, too. I'll change it."

Apparently, he does not feel satisfied with my answer. He repeats his gripe, this time adding flourishes with his right arm. He is leaning against the wall with his legs on a stool in front of him and his left arm rests on the table. Encouraged by my agreement, he embellishes his description of my behavior and emphasizes his frustration, how wronged he's been.

I've been working the bread dough—adding flour—for several minutes now, and the six-pound, six-loaf mound is nearly ready to put into a bowl to rise. I feel the satisfaction again, the sense of economy of making six loaves at a time. My oven is small, and all six bake at once in less time than only two loaves would take. I save propane, which we have to charter here in a single-engine plane from Anchorage, 160 miles east. With the time I save, I get to transplant more wild raspberries to cross with the domestic ones, making larger, more flavorful berries for my raspberry rhubarb pies. Or, I get to turn more of the rich brown earth to plant edible pod Chinese peas that I couldn't afford to buy in town when I lived there, or potatoes and carrots that grow sweet in this cold soil. Every minute of the summer daylight, I am drawn to my garden when it's not time to take the boat to check our setnet downstream.

My concentration is broken. I hear his voice behind me. I say for the third (or is it the fourth time?): "Yes, I heard you and I understand your frustration. I'm sorry. I will change." But this time I add, "I heard you. I agreed to deal with it. I don't want to hear it again. I have heard enough. Please don't bring it up again."

Behind me he sits still for a moment, but the pressure is too much. He starts in at me again. I no longer hear his words. I interpret and hear, "BiiitchBitchBitchBitchBitch, Bitch, Bitch, breath, BiiitchBitchBitchBitchBitch, breath, BiiiitchBi..." and the noise continues behind me. I think about my ex-husband, an ex for only about a year—not nearly long enough to make up for the seven years of intimidating me through incessant bitching, yelling, isolating me with no transportation 150 miles from the road system, shoving me around, bringing his girlfriends to stay with me and holding a gun on me when I didn't behave the way he wanted me to. He always said that I could leave anytime I wanted to, but he was going with me. When we first got together, I used to laugh at that. After awhile I didn't laugh at anything.

The night he held the loaded .38 on my forehead, I was free. In the middle of the room full of people—in the middle of this room, in fact—I'd told him. "Go ahead, it would be so much better than this." And I realized I meant it. What could he do to me then? I was free.

So really—really—I didn't need this. The drone of this other man—another one—continued behind me.

Someone, and it must have been me, picked up the heavy mound of dough and hurled it across the room at the mouth that wouldn't stop.

He sat perfectly still.

He told me later that it was like in slow motion. He saw the mound leave my hands and start toward him. As it came across the room, the momentum carried the different parts of its mass in different directions and it developed appendages all over, reaching out like an amoebae.

He had been a gunner on a recon helicopter in Vietnam when the United States was really in the war, in 1965. He had been shot down five times and been shot three times. He faced the dough unflinchingly, probably hoping for contact.

The six-pound, many-armed mound flew across the kitchen and dining area toward him. Someone, and it must have been me, stood still at the counter—watching.

Six inches in front of his long-beaked face, the six-loaf, six-pound many-armed mound flew apart, flew in two and hit the golden log wall behind him on either side. He sat perfectly still, looking at me, the bread dough oozing down the wall on either side of him.

Someone—it was me—said, "I told you I'd heard enough."

And he sat perfectly still while I scooped the dough from the wall beside him, before I put it in the oiled bowl to rise.

Terri D. Doyle

ROSELYN MARIE AND HER NEW HAIR

Deep Chestnut Brown, is what the box called the latest shade of "Beautiful Hair Colors for Women" when she decided to change her image again. Burnt three-day-old coffee is more what it looked like when she was done. She had followed most of the directions on the box faithfully, just as she had all the other times she discovered a new and exciting woman within herself. This time the new woman had emerged from a cocoon of Jean Harlow blonde into the much more mysterious world of the Veronica Lake brunette. The brittle, three inch long hairs that rested around the bathtub plug didn't seem to matter to Roselyn Marie much more than the nuisance they created when they blocked the little holes forcing the tarnish colored water to pool up when it should have been draining. As she looked into the steam-edged mirror when she stepped out of the tub, she saw only that being a brunette made her hair look shorter and more closely cut to her squat little neck.

Roselyn Marie moved over toward her closet and stood with her tiny fat hands resting on the round gold-tone door handles as she pondered her choices. Did she want the purple and white checkered housecoat or the tangerine orange and white tropical flower housecoat? She pulled out three or four other housecoats and tossed them onto her unmade bed. One by one, she undid the long zipper on the front of each cotton dress and held them against her stump of a body. She admired the way her new hair played with the different colors in the bright materials. She finally selected a sunny yellow and white polka dot design that had its zipper hidden behind a flap of golden yellow ribbon. She especially liked this housecoat because it had big white plastic buttons sewn onto the two-inch wide ribbon.

As she was putting the other dresses back into her crowded closet she thought about the perfect accessory for her new look. Roselyn Marie walked over to her hall closet. It was so much easier to get to since removing the door a few months ago. Now she just had to part the dark blue and green plastic beads that rained down from the top of the doorjamb to the gold shag carpet. The shelves were stuffed full of hats and scarves and purses with the excess hanging and falling into little piles on top of a rainbow assortment of colored shoes. She immediately slipped her tiny square feet into a practical pair of white low-heeled pumps and balanced her back against the wall for a more comfortable view of her hats.

All her hats were on the shelf directly in front of her and she started grabbing through them. The fact that they were all black didn't discourage Roselyn Marie from trying on all sorts of different styles: the Spanish dancer hat the with little black pom-poms dangling all around the brim; the tight little box hat, the kind that reminded her of Jackie Kennedy in mourning; the small, folded velvet headband with the black netted veil holding little rhinestones over her eyes. None of them looked just right, but only because they covered up too much of her hair. No, Roselyn Marie decided that the perfect accessory was the opalescent yellow scarf up on the next shelf.

She could see it peeking out just behind a taped up old shoe box filled with an assortment of decorative gloves. Since Roselyn Marie stood almost five foot and one inch tall, the shelf that held her scarf hung high above her head. She tried to hoist herself up to the next shelf by balancing her left foot on the lowest shelf above the floor. She slid her right foot sideways and back against the doorjamb, then pushed off with a huff of air trying to catapult her body up toward the higher shelf. Her short round fingers clutched inches below their intended target causing her body's weight to force her left foot back off the lower shelf and onto the floor with a loud smack. The rest of her body quickly followed with only her knee slamming into the edge of the shelf as she fell.

She really wanted that scarf now that she had skinned up her knee and knocked down the shelf, spilling all the black little hats on top of the rainbow of shoes. As she struggled in the pile of accessories to get up, she remembered that she had an old pair of black knee-hi stockings rolled up in her work purse. She could just as well wear those as the suntan colored ones she was planning on. Black, she decided, would cover up any residual bruising that might come from her mishap in the closet. Black also made her calves look thinner, and since thin is sexier than fat, she knew she had found the right color in hosiery to go with her new hair.

Roselyn Marie darted into her guest room to slide the step-ladder out from under the small twin bed. She had to struggle and tug just a little to get the ladder to maneuver around the broken slats that hung under the box springs. The more she wiggled the ladder back and forth, the more she seemed to wedge it around the frayed edges of a slat. All she wanted was to get her beautiful scarf down from the closet shelf so her outfit would be complete; instead she was having a tug-of-war for her step-ladder with a dilapidated twin bed.

She sat back to survey her situation and decided that, with just the right leverage, she could extract the ladder with one big tug. So she wiggled her body up on her folded knees and rested her entirety on bent feet and ankles. Having secured her balance, she reached forward and down, grasping the edge of the ladder with both of her fists and yanked with all her strength. Not only did she successfully remove the step-ladder from the clutches of the old bed, but she managed to throw herself backwards almost all the way out into the hallway. She considered this to be a stroke of good fortune since it placed her that much closer to her goal.

She arrived back in front of her closet and scouted around on the floor for some solid ground to balance the step-ladder on. This time she just had to push her red and white polka dot pumps and some gold and silver slip-ons out of the way to position the front legs of the ladder up against where the lower shelf had been standing. She used her right foot as a mop to clear the area under and behind the back legs, so she could test the ladder for stability. Once convinced, she confidently climbed the three steps necessary to fully see the shelf that hid her perfect accessory to complete her transformation into a mysterious and seductive brunette. Roselyn Marie envisioned how she was going to tie the yellow opalescent material around her neck. Or maybe she would wrap it across her shoulders, or weave it over her hair and under her ears to give her a more youthful appearance. If she tied it through her hair she could carry the long scarf ends back over her shoulders and let them drape down over her chest. The idea of her chest playing peek-a-boo behind a sheer yellow scarf swinging as she walked down the street, brought that carved crevice of a smile back onto her face. As her imaginary self danced down the street taunting all those who walked past in her mind, her hand reached the yellow scarf.

She pulled back on the scarf using the wistful sighs from her daydream as the driving force behind her movements. The prized accessory flowed effortlessly out of the tangled insanity of overflowing scarves, arching upwards in a weightless flight of freedom. Roselyn Marie snapped her wrist with all the skill of a belly dancer and lead the scarf to float across her neck and down toward her feet. With success in her round little fingertips, she lowered herself down the step-ladder, waving her left foot toward the ground before finally stepping with all her weight back onto the floor of her hallway.

Since it was very important to Roselyn Marie to see how she would look as a new woman, she quickly shoved the ladder into the accessory closet and did her best to skip toward her bedroom, limping slightly on her scraped and bruised knee. She grabbed her purse as she dropped onto her rumpled bed and started to rummage through it to find her black knee-his. After two or three swipes through the bulging contents of her self-proclaimed survival kit, she decided it would be easier to just dump the purse upside-down onto her bed and grab the black ball of nylons. Roselyn latched onto the stockings and started to unroll them as she leaned back to face her legs. As she wadded the stocking leg up between her thumbs and forefingers, she kicked off her pumps to expose her naked feet. She bent over and pointed her toes into the opening of her stockings and worked the black nylon up her legs, first her left foot then her right. As she reached her knees with each nylon, she would quickly pull her fingers out of the tops and let them snap back against her translucent white calves as she slipped her feet back into her shoes.

With one fluid motion, Roselyn Marie lifted herself up off her bed and moved toward the full-length mirror mounted on the side of her chest of drawers. She held her crowning scarf gently in her hand so as not to wrinkle it. Roselyn Marie paused only for a moment before she slung the scarf over her bangs dividing them from the rest of her hair, and pulled the scarf tightly down behind her ears. She bent forward at the waist and tossed her frazzled hair off her neck so she could tie the ends of the scarf together without tying up her hair. Once she was happy with the knot, she whipped her head back as if she could snap her hair into the perfect seductive style. As she carried the scarf ends over her shoulders, she twirled around on the toes of her right foot, pretending to be a ballerina performing the Dance of the Swans.

Regaining her balance after her dizzying dance, Roselyn Marie opened her eyes and saw her miraculous transformation into a beautiful and sultry brunette. She suffered very little, if she were to count the scrape on her knee, in her successful attempt to change her life. And even if her chest didn't play peek-a-boo behind an opalescent yellow scarf as she walked down the street, she could pretend to be winking behind a curled swatch of brown hair that had fallen over her right eye.

She looked at herself in the mirror, winked seductively then tossed back her hair as she started toward the front door. It was time to show the world the new and seductive Roselyn Marie. As she left her house for her afternoon walk, she started humming off-key "The Girl from Ipanema."

Brenda Kleinfelder

WINTER AIR

I'm suffocating in a tiny Alaskan town
choking on winter gossip
gasping for air in my fish bowl privacy
strangling myself as I twist tighter
in the web of secrets I swore not to tell

I cross paths with the same people at least five times a day
in this tiny Alaskan town where stalking is hard to prove
and forgiveness comes in the form of forgetfulness

I've become an asthmatic begging for a deep breath
of rejuvenating crisp clean oxygen
to soften my opinions
about people's problems I know nothing about
oh, I attend those winter potlucks
where piping hot gossip is eagerly brought
and rumors are heartily spread onto home-made bread
and bitter coffee is sweetened by someone else's tears

I have been there and eaten my share
my Thanksgiving gluttony of people and pain
but my belt is too tight
I push back from the table before the dessert
eager to unlatch my buckle and begin my fast
and take a deep drag off the cold winter air

Karen A. Tschannen

SHORT STORY

   so this is how it ends
not with a look of damage
only a silent bruise of surprise
staining your face
no tangle of leads and tubes
no repeated victories
measured in beats like the metronome
set to practice **Ein Heldenleben**
for our daughter's debut

   as such things go
I've been assured
it was a good death
but I know
its red explosion
moved the ground
half a world away
even now
after all this time
sensitive seismographs
still measure aftershocks
distant people
do not feel

   I see you
going on before me
watching for lion
in the long grass
in the tall grass
like the hero
in a Hemingway story
but you flushed your lion
when I wasn't even watching
before the gunbearer
could come up

Tracy Philpot

THE INFIDELITY OF BIRDS

Last night loyal dogs fell
from the sky instead of these birds,
jagged swindlers,
dropping down for seed and gossip at our feeder.
Inside we are not so much humane
as we are voyeurs, videotaping the holes
lying somewhere between the trees
and these glassy windows.

Inattention makes you believe in birds,
assuming nature makes them behave.
I thought their hearts too tiny
to hold much more than lightness
and blood. But sometimes
during the last chanes of dusk
I understand their flying towards something darker,
the pornographic rush to what we don't have.

In Oregon, I heard of a merganser diving
under the water, holding himself
not like a lover, but under the water
among the vines, reflections of trees rippling
like houseboats above him, in case he should reconsider.
I love unusual endings,
his interpretation of flight.

I weave pictures into the walls of my room,
steal the birds' bits of string and hair.
Who's to say trash doesn't make good mementos?

There's no bird's song in here—screeching and bones
erasing some people we lose
to the sky. Romance in birds
gives them an edge on the personal world,
the violence of not coming home
with dinner. I guess it's messy for them to go on
flying as they do above the clock towers.
Hell, they can't tell time.

Birds are enormously more obvious than we are
when they have affairs,
visiting other nests in the same suit
as the real spouse,
tending another's eggs—
I am hungry now as they start singing
country-western.
But how often can we count on this?

Tracy Philpot

THE HOLIDAY OF ESCAPE

Imagine the colors of independence, black
against which spires burst forth
as if we stand on the deck of a warship
watching for some familiar sign of the future.
I've never sailed. I'm not rich
and I don't want a husband.

Even if I've loved you this way once
it will never happen again.
The aqua city floats by at twilight.

My best friend dreams she understands holidays:
skies like brief finger-paintings,
children we name but don't have,
black and white foreign films, the coolness we lack.
I hate to say I love my country
but I've traveled.

I re-live every relationship I've ever had
at the same time. Figure this to be
freedom or isolation.
I hear thunder in the other room
and have no memory.

On the day my country's free
nuns disappear from monasteries,
a Russian sailor runs wild on an American beach
with a knife and a flag,
a single man moves into our old house
and a doctor tells my friend he can cure her.

You came to me like an idea
I had been wrestling with for months.
You brought small lights for the room,
and when your mouth opened I heard
the quiet waves outside bringing back
the privacy of lost things,
the unsuccessful differences.

T. L. Scott

THE BAR MAIDS OF HAGA MARI

Crooked houses line the road
like houses of cards,
struggling against one another
for support, ready to collapse in
the slightest breeze, at the clap of hands.

The narrow road follows
the railroad, which follows
the same course as the Han.
All three, the street, the rails, the river,
the same, a dark and mottled gray.

The only bright color, the verdant
mountains reclining fromt the water
and brothels. In a landscape turned
monochrome, the sun begins to set
like a deflating orange balloon.

Then with suddenness and jarring,
like variegated butterflies from dun cocoons,
come the flowers of the village,
the girls of the bars, their voices
high with excitement and regret.

This is their best hour,
before soldiers become sloppy
with drunkenness, before locals
begin to haggle over prices.
They are fresh, graceful and as lithe

as dancers. They go with painted faces
and satin dresses which cling
like leaves on wet stones
along the river's edge. They will lie
between cracked walls with duty and complacency.

But for the moment, they are free.
Later they will do all
that's possible, to make men want them.
For lonely soldiers, the invitation
is always open, dance cards are never full.

T. L. Scott

NEIGHBORS

For Mike Ryan, wherever you are

We sit on his front stoop,
spread the Sunday paper across two laps
and titter at the funnies.
It is late September,
and the marigolds have gone brown.
The rubbish left inside
is closed behind us.
Delilah, he says,
will be back tomorrow.
I smile politely and stare at the white
mushrooms that grow beside the steps.
She'll bring Phoebe, he tells me,
and groceries and drown us
with kisses. The curve in the road
makes the wind rise
like a wave, he says.
I smile again. I know no wife,
no child will return
and I believe nothing.

He says the only mail he gets is bills
and one letter that leaves him
cold-cocked. I wash his stacked dishes,
I see him through
the steamy window. He stands out back,
checks his worm bed, chews a wild onion.
he says he'd rather be outside
than hear the phone
ring and it's the same old lady
who has reached the wrong number.

M. Otis Beard

Amphibian Hand

He spoke a jagged language that no one understood
and camped out on the open palms of strangers
In his pocket was a lump of coal
Christmas present from the cracked vellum years
that had rolled off his back and gurgled in his throat.

Magnets frightened him. The aluminum foil hat he wore
repelled their evil waves and kept him safe
Safe from probing, safe from changes
safe from eyes that tracked him, seeking wine
safe from machines that craved his salty blood.

Dumpsters held discarded secrets, held the scales
fallen from the eyes of sages far from shore
In shopping carts he stacked lost things he'd found
philosopher's stones and rooster's eggs
Dead Sea scrolls and amphorae of Greek fire.

If you asked, he could or would not tell his name
or when he was born, or where, or why
He spoke a jagged language that no one understood
and shuffled, new lungs choking on thin, dry air
up from the ancient sea to live on land at last.

M. Otis Beard

INSPECTED BY

To say that Cleveland Marsh was rather fussy would be akin to saying that the interior of the sun was rather warm. Cleveland was more than fussy, he was pathologically neat.

He was also hideously wealthy, having inherited an immense shipping fortune from his overachieving father. In spite of this, he insisted on doing many of his own household chores, since the maids either could or would not perform certain tasks to his extremely rigid specifications.

A case in point was the laundry. Despite the detailed instructions he had given to the household staff, a surprise visit to the laundry room deep in the bowels of his enormous mansion confirmed his suspicions that a bit of corner-cutting was taking place down there. Concealed in a cupboard, he watched in horror as the maid on duty carelessly tossed a handful of detergent into the washer without first weighing the laundry, calculating the amount of detergent necessary, and measuring precisely that amount into the little compartment on the top of the machine. To make matters worse, she took wet laundry out of the washer and shoved it willy-nilly into the dryer without bothering to fold it first. Granted, she did an excellent job of folding it after it was dry, and so Cleveland allowed her to remain in his employ; but from that day forward he tended to the laundry himself.

As further evidence of his fussiness, it may be noted that the clothing Cleveland so meticulously washed and dried was not his own, but that of the household staff. The impeccable Mr. Marsh would never be caught dead wearing the same garment twice. Each morning he arrayed himself in crisp new finery straight from the tailor's shop downtown, hand delivered to his home in crackling brown paper packages. When he was finished wearing a suit of clothing, it was whisked away to be given to some local charity or other. Thanks to this small kindness, the town in which Cleveland Marsh lived harbored a number of homeless alcoholics who could have easily made Mr. Blackwell's best-dressed list.

One morning as he was getting dressed, Cleveland noticed something that greatly ruffled his morning calm. The trousers he had just stepped into had a long black thread hanging from the outside seam of the left leg. Frowning, he grasped the offending fiber between thumb and index finger and yanked sharply. Unfortunately, the thread failed to break, and Cleveland found himself face to face with an eight-inch gap along the seam of his trousers, through which the pallid flesh of his thigh peeked out at him.

When he had regained enough of his lost composure to speak, he summoned his valet.

"Walter," he said, pointing to the hole in his trousers, "this will not do. I want you to call my tailor this instant. Tell him to send another pair of trousers right away, and make sure they're of a better quality than this . . . this . . . ."

"Egregious example of lackadaisical craftsmanship?" offered Walter, who had majored in English Lit.

"Yes. Precisely," snapped Cleveland. "Tell him it's just this sort of thing that's sending this country to the dogs."

When the new pair of trousers arrived, Cleveland looked them over thoroughly before putting them on. They were manufactured by a company he had never heard of, but they seemed to be a good product, and the stitching was perfect. He thrust his hands into the pockets to get the feel of them, and his right hand encountered a small square of paper. Puzzled, he pulled it out and examined it. It was about two inches by two inches, and printed on it in perfectly centered boldface text were the words 'Inspected by No. 17.'

How odd, thought Cleveland. Somewhere in the world is a person completely devoted to making sure that my trousers are in order.

The idea gave him a strange little twinge of pride. He felt a certain kinship with this inspector seventeen. Clearly, this was someone who, like him, realized the importance of attention to detail. If only there were more people like that in the world, perhaps it would be a better place in which to live.

Absorbed by this thought, he moved automatically towards the nearest wastebasket to throw the scrap of paper away, but some sudden impulse stopped him at the last moment and he tucked it carefully into his wallet instead.

The next morning brought another pair of perfect trousers, and another square of paper from inspector seventeen. So did the morning after that, and the next morning, and the morning after that. This daily assurance that someone in the world besides himself still cared about a job well done was like a campfire to Cleveland's great marshmallow of a heart. He positively glowed at each day's discovery of the buried treasure in his pocket. For this reason he simply could not bring himself to throw the scraps of paper out, and so he ordered a large leather-bound stamp collecting book and took to pasting the things neatly into it.

The weeks and months rolled by, and Cleveland began having oddly pleasant dreams at night. One in particular recurred again and again, with minor variations. A shadowy presence seemed to be standing behind him, watching over him. He sensed that the presence was female, and felt a vast benign warmth radiating from her. The smell of roses, a smell that he associated with his long-dead mother, tickled his nostrils. He would try to turn and face the presence, but somehow she always managed to remain just out of his view. At some point she would press something into his hand and whisper the words "I am with you," in his ear. He would look down to see what sort of talisman he had received, only to find the now familiar square of paper and suddenly realize that he was dreaming. This realization inevitably propelled him quickly upward through the dark waters of sleep towards consciousness, and he would awake with one hand clenched tightly, as if to pull the dream-paper along with him into the bright world of morning. It always depressed him slightly to find that his hand was empty, and his sense of loss was compounded by the fact that he could never quite recall the dream or the nature of the object he had failed to extract from it.

His attention began to drift in his waking hours. He spent more and more time gazing at nothing with a vague little smile on his face, oblivious to his surroundings. He had always been rather good with numbers, but now they seemed to jumble themselves around in his head. One morning at breakfast he was amazed to find before him a huge plate heaped high with well over a dozen quivering fried eggs. The cook, distraught, insisted that he had ordered them.

"You say gimme seventeen eggs," she said. "I ask you how many eggs you want for breakfast, and you say seventeen. I don't make no trouble, Mr. Cleveland, you know that. You want seventeen eggs for breakfast, that's okay with me. I just cook, I don't ask no questions."

It was a few days after this incident that Cleveland had what was, hands-down, the single most distressing moment of his life. He had just finished getting dressed, and the corners of his mouth curved upward slightly in anticipation as he slipped his right hand into his pocket . . . and found nothing.

His puzzlement turned to panic as he explored more carefully and still came up empty-handed. He turned the pocket inside out; there was nothing there. *She's gone,* he thought wildly, and a medley of feelings played across his mind too quickly to be influenced by rational thought, a rapid succession of emotional sixteenth-notes crying loss, anger, fear, confusion, and despair. She had abandoned him, she had quit her job, she was ill, injured, dying, dead.

He nearly choked with relief and delight when he found the precious square of paper . . . in his left hand pocket.

There was no longer any denying it. Cleveland Marsh had fallen deeply, hopelessly, irrationally and irrevocably in love.

It wasn't a pining sort of love, although the object of his affections was absent. The mechanical details of sex had always seemed rather unnecessarily messy to him anyway. No, things were perfect just the way they were. The proof of her love for him came with every pair of trousers he wore.

And if there was an extra bit of spring in his step, if he was a trifle more tolerant with his employees, if a smile came to his lips just a little more quickly than before, it was because Cleveland Marsh was a man fulfilled.

Ted Herlinger

MUSHROOMS

Shortly after closing time Saturday evening, while sitting at the counter funneling black pepper into the little glass shakers, Ruby turned her face to sneeze. She thought she caught a glimpse of something peculiar under the corner table.

"Oh, Bob?" she chuckled, envisioning the sour grimace that would follow her suggestion he'd overlooked a scrap when he swept the floor. Sliding off the stool, she waddled to the booth and stooped, studying the thing for a moment before slumping to her knees and extending her hand toward it. When it appeared to shrink away from her fingers, a shiver wriggled from the top of her scalp to the base of her spine. Flinching, she bumped her head on the underside of the table and tumbled backwards with a thump into the middle of the floor. Bob scrambled through the swinging door, stopped short and stared open-mouthed at her. "Wha . . . what's the matter, Ruby?" he frowned. "What's happened?"

"Take a look at that!" she gasped, pointing a trembling finger toward the table. "Take a look under there and tell me what you see."

Bob glanced from Ruby to the table and back to Ruby. "What is it?" he glared. "What did I miss?"

"Take a look!" Ruby insisted, shaking her head. "It ain't what you think. I don't know what it is. Look at it!"

Bob knelt and peered into the dark corner.

"You see it?" Ruby asked, rubbing the top of her head. "You see what I mean?"

"I'll be God damned!" Bob groaned as he crawled under the table. "Looks like a mushroom!" Backing out into the light, he stood up and stared at the brown lump in his hand. "It wasn't there when I swept up. I would'a seen it." He scratched his head. "I'll be God damned! Growin' right outta the floor. What's a mushroom doin' growin' outta the floor? Never saw nothin' like it."

"I swear it moved," Ruby said, rising to her feet. "When I

went for it. Liked to scared me half to death."

"Well, it ain't movin' now," Bob sighed. "But I never saw nothin' like it."

"What you got, there?" Mel asked, strolling through the swinging door, wiping his hands on his apron.

"Mushroom," said Bob, nodding toward the corner booth. "Was under the table, there."

"Is that all?" Mel grinned. "To hear you two jabberin' out there, I thought you'd found a cockroach or somethin'." He shook his head. "Prob'ly missed it when you swept up."

"Nope," Bob shrugged, knitting his brow. "It was growin' under there."

"Oh, horseshit!" Mel laughed. "I'd have to be goofy as you to believe that."

"Take a look at it," said Bob. He handed it toward Mel. "Never saw nothin' like it before. Did you?"

"Just a mushroom," Mel smiled, shaking his head. "We got a couple flats of 'em where that one came from. In the walk-in." He glanced at the wall clock. "Now, if you're done messin' around, I'd like to get outta here some time tonight."

Bob knit his brow and looked from the mushroom to Ruby. Shrugging her shoulders, Ruby waddled back to the counter, straddled a stool and resumed filling the pepper shakers. Bob followed Mel as he turned and stepped through the swinging door.

Later, as Mel was locking the back door, Bob sat down next to Ruby at the counter. "They ain't the same," he whispered.

"You're sure?" Ruby asked, cocking her head. "How can you be sure?"

"Shh!" he hissed, glancing toward the swinging door. Opening his palm, he showed her a plump white mushroom. "This one's from the walk-in. It ain't anything like the other one. Other one was...I don't know...had little bumps on it, like, and it was brown."

"What'd you do with it?" Ruby frowned. "The other one, I mean."

"Put it down the disposal," Bob winked, watching the swinging door. He closed his hand around the mushroom. "I don't care what he says. Wasn't there when I swept up. I would'a seen it." He rubbed his chin with the back of his hand. "Anyway, you saw it. It was growin' outta the floor. They ain't the same."

"He better not catch you takin' that outta here," Ruby whispered, nodding at Bob's hand.

Bob opened his hand, stared at the mushroom for a moment, and popped it in his mouth.

"I hope you washed that," Ruby shuddered.

Bob grinned as he chewed the mushroom. Striding through the swinging door, Mel flipped the light switches off. "Guess that about does it," he said. "See you guys Monday, bright and early."

"Bright and early," Bob smiled, wiping his mouth with the back of his hand.

Sunday morning, as Pastor Larson was proclaiming the righteousness of Job's forbearance, Ruby's head slumped forward and her eyes snapped open. Emerging from a foggy daze, she glanced sideways. Nobody seemed to have noticed her lapse, so she relaxed.

"Behold," the minister intoned, "this is the joy of his way and out of the earth shall others grow."

Ruby twitched in her seat as a shudder, sparked by the word "grow," pulsed down her back. She sneaked another sidelong peek at her neighbors, who sat like mannequins, their passive eyes fixed on the altar.

"You see," the preacher continued," throughout all his many trials, Job steadfastly acknowledged God's justice and omnipotence. Who among us can say as much? Who among us has not been tried and as a result, demanded, 'Why me, God?' Who among us?" He paused, scanning the expanse of faces. "Behold," he resumed, "this is the joy of his way and . . . " As Ruby's eyes drooped, her head settled backwards and she drifted again into a warm, peaceful mist, light feathery clouds cradling her, like a sea of airy comforters. Streams of dazzling white light cascaded from a halo high above her. A slight movement somewhere below startled her and she looked down just in time to see, shooting up out of the clouds toward her like a rocket, a blistered brown mushroom cap atop a thick meaty shaft.

"Out of the earth shall others grow," a deep bass voice thundered.

"No! No mushrooms!" she screamed, her head sagging forward.

As if synchronized, every face in the congregation, eyes wide with astonishment, spun in her direction. Pastor Larson, furrowing his brow, frowned at her. Her face flushed, Ruby clasped her hands in her lap, stared down at her feet and remained petrified in that position until, following the benediction, she arose and yielded to the interminable procession of worshipers plodding past the minister. Even then she seemed incapable of lifting her gaze from the floor, terrified of meeting the bitter glares she felt were being directed at her.

"Are you all right, Ruby?" Pastor Larson whispered, as he touched her hand.

"Just pooped, I guess," Ruby muttered, still staring downward. "Sorry," she added. Clutching her handbag close to her side, she waddled down the narthex and out the door.

Ruby's occasional spells of shallow sleep Sunday night were tormented by recurrent visions of foul, spongeous mushroom caps snaking up out of sink drains on gnarled and swollen stalks. When her alarm jangled, shattering the early morning darkness, drenched in sweat and heavy with exhaustion, she rolled toward the wall and pulled the covers over her head. Fatigue, however, had no power over years of routine, and as the first blush of light tinged the brow of the mountains, she was stepping in the back door of the restaurant.

"Morning, Ruby," Bob grinned, as he sat shredding potatoes into a large pot.

"Morning, Ruby," Mel nodded. "Have a nice day off?"

"Oh, I guess," Ruby sighed. She pulled an apron off a hook and wrapped it around her waist. "How about you?"

"Can't complain," Mel said, shoving a pan of bacon into an oven. "Can't complain."

Waddling to the walk-in, Ruby pulled the door open and stepped inside. She lifted a case of eggs, lugged them out and set them on the floor. As she turned to close the walk-in door, she thought she caught a glimpse of something peculiar under one of the sinks.

"Oh, Lord," she murmured under her breath, a shiver squirming down her spine. Bob looked away as Ruby glanced at him. Waddling to the sink, she stooped, slumped to her knees and extended her hand toward it. It didn't shrink away from her when she grasped it firmly in her fingers. Rising, she held it up to the light, bending and twisting it. Covered with tiny bumps, it was mottled brown and springy, made of plastic or rubber. She shook her head.

"What you got, there?" Mel asked, strolling toward her.

"Mushroom," Ruby smiled, dropping it down the drain. "Bob must've missed it when he swept up."

Staring open-mouthed at Ruby and shaking his head, Bob continued shredding potatoes. Ruby turned on the cold water. She switched the garbage disposal on. The grinding clatter was peaceful to Ruby, like sweet music.

Rob Lecrone

THE HEADED AND THE GUTTED

When Ike's wife and daughter came back to him, they came back as a dream, wispy and unreal. They were phantoms already the night Ike drank at Cave Zero with Crazy Eye Jack, the night before Jack's accident, and they were phantoms still two months later when they swam salmon-like before Ike's eyes, halfway through his shift, at 6 a.m. or so, while he worked the header. Ike slid salmon after salmon across the slime on the counter into the machine where, as his foot pressed the pedal on the floor, a v-shaped blade slammed down. The severed heads shot down a chute into a metal tote in the back of the building while the salmon continued down the line toward freezing. Swoosh clunk, swoosh clunk the blade slammed down, and Ike had to be fast to keep the rest of the line moving. If he was too fast, though, he would wear out everybody down the line. Sometimes you had to so you could weed out the slackers.

Ike knew Crazy Eye Jack from the plant where Jack had worked the header before the job became Ike's. As far back as when Ike was a slimer on the line, spooning the bloodlines from the spines of the headed and the gutted, Jack had worked it. Quick and talented with any blade, Crazy Eye Jack headed at a terrific pace when he wanted to. His speech was the only thing slow about him, but it was as loud as the sound of the header cutting through fish. Crazy Eye Jack's talent let him work as fast with the knife as with the machine.

That night Ike drank with Jack at Cave Zero was the night after Carolyn took Ike's daughter and left. That night Ike saw Jack cut a man in a brawl. The knife sliced across a forearm and blood spurted out. Jack walked calmly out the back and disappeared. Ike watched the bartender clutch a towel against the fountain of blood and scream for one of the barmaids to call an ambulance. Ike wasn't thinking about Jack or the man bleeding or the bartender or the barmaid. He finished his beer before leaving.

The day after Jack cut the man in the bar, Jack cut his right hand off in the header machine. The blood flowed and Jack's crazy eyes spun in unison for the first time as his face grew pale. He knocked the knife off the heading table and it clanged on the floor.

Ike watched the hand on the floor, a spider struggling to turn over while dying on its back. Dante Rivera and an old man called Joe helped Crazy Eye Jack into the office while a beefy kid with about four whiskers on his chin yelled for the Chief.

Ike picked up the hand and put it in a plastic bag. Somebody shoveled ice into the bag while he held it. Blood spread through the ice. It looked like a bag of cherry snowcone. A pool of blood on the floor flowed into the drain to mix with the blood of salmon. Ike bent down and took up Jack's knife.

After Ike had the knife, his eyes settled on the metal totes filled with fish. Dante and Joe had Jack in Chief's office. All the workers were gathered around the glass walls of the office. Ike tried to worry about Jack but could only worry about when his wife and daughter would come back. He didn't want to think about it.

"All right!" he yelled. "There's still work to be done! Break's over!"

Slowly the workers streamed back to the slime line. One skinny college kid puked in a tote of fish heads before punching out on the time clock and walking away.

"Here," Ike said, handing the bag with Jack's hand in it to Andy, a wrinkled drunk with burst veins weaving about his nose. "Take this in the office and see if they need anything." He handed Andy the knife. "Take this, too."

Ike fitted his hand into the leather strap designed to prevent accidents like Crazy Eye Jack's and chopped the head off the first salmon. Swoosh clunk. His hand reached out for a salmon and slid it into the machine. Swoosh clunk. He grabbed a salmon and slid it under the blade. Swoosh clunk. He focused on the monotonous sound to avoid thinking. Another tote was brought in. Swoosh clunk. Swoosh clunk. Swoosh clunk.

For two months, Ike was able to immerse himself in the sound of the header while he was at work, avoiding thoughts about his wife and daughter who had still not returned to him. He'd heard nothing and had lost the ability to picture them perfectly in his mind. When he was not at work, he could not help thinking.

Two months after Jack lost his hand, while Ike was standing at the header, his wife and daughter intruded on the sound of the machine. Like the past two summers working at the plant, the summer of his wife's leaving and of the hand was not filled with enough sleep, but when Ike did sleep he dreamed. Of course there were the fish. The long nights coupled with the fish added a strangeness to the drives home from work. Ike would see salmon swimming in the asphalt. All the mountains were giant salmon rising. The empty house was a stream he waded through.

Hallucinations and strange sleeping and waking dreams went along with the swirling state of mind that Ike sunk into when he worked the long salmon hours, and of course there were the fish. But there were other things, and this night two other things in particular. Swoosh clunk. Carolyn and Angie flashed across his mind, his wife's eyes staring at him through the light of a candle. Swoosh clunk swoosh. The candlelight snuffed between the fingers of a floating, disembodied hand, not the gnarly, arachnid hand of Crazy Eye Jack but the broad, stumpy hand that was Ike's. Angie, Ike's daughter, floated back into a corridor of shadow receding into her mother's eyes. The fish swam through the carpet. A stream ran out the door and fly fishermen lined the banks casting their lines. Swoosh clunk. A hand came off, going down the shoot and into a tote. Something fought on Ike's line but he could not reel it in.

Chief came up and put his hand on Ike's shoulder and Ike's wife and daughter turned into salmon and swam upstream away from him.

"Okay," Chief said, "break."

"Break!" Ike yelled and took his hand out of the leather strap.

He was glad to be away from the header. He drank his coffee and stood by the soda machine. The noise of the header had relaxed him with its hypnotizing sound since Crazy Eye Jack went to the hospital the night after Ike's wife took his daughter and left, but the header could not help him anymore. He crumpled up his coffee cup and tossed it in the garbage.

He went into the bathroom. After he'd washed his hands and studied the lines in his face, he pulled out a crumpled picture from his pocket. He'd been carrying it around and the lines were getting deep so that he was having trouble seeing his little girl's features. He'd have to start carrying a new one. A corner was torn down by his wife's left foot. The dog wasn't even in the picture and neither was Ike.

Ike walked back into the break room. He was surprised to see that Crazy Eye Jack was there. All the workers were gathered around him trying not to look at the place where his hand had been. Ike couldn't help but look. For some reason, he had expected that if Jack came back, it would be with his right hand Frankenstein stitched on. He'd hoped that his effort to save the hand would have been successful. Now he saw that he hadn't helped anything.

Even if he had, he thought, it would not have worked out.

He imagined what it would have been like then, if the hand had been surgically reattached. He could picture it very well. Jack would motion to Ike with the hand. It would seem an odd thing. From where Ike was standing, the hand would look plastic, and Ike would walk over and shake it. He would feel that it was worse than plastic, flesh and not flesh, cold and weak. The fingers would twitch and Jack would not be able to squeeze.

"How are you?" Ike would ask, and Jack would look as if he

knew his hand was worthless. Ike supposed that Crazy Eye Jack would clear his throat slowly and say in his loud, yawning voice, "Well... they thought they did well." His crazy eye would move all around.

"Yeah," Ike would say. He would know what Crazy Eye Jack meant.

A few months later, in the middle of the winter, Ike learned from a magazine article that missing limbs become phantom limbs, that the brain remaps and feeling returns as if the nonexistent places were still a part of the person. Ike read about people without arms who still felt them swinging as they walked and about a man who could feel his missing hand grasping things and picking them up. Never, Ike thought, would the feelings disappear.

Krys Holmes

EATING ALASKA

My father raised us in the mountains so we could learn to love the unexpected, and my mother raised us near the sea so we could come to know a power greater than ourselves. My dad was a college teacher in Montana, so we lived there during the school year. We lived with my grandmother on the shores of central California in the summer, and by that syncopation of a life stretched taut between livestock yards and sardine factories I learned to appreciate the world by smell.

The smell of beef cattle in the lot on a midsummer prairie scorcher hits your nose like a barn door. It's a flat, obliterating odor so powerful you don't get a chance to like or dislike it, you just try to breathe around it. Fish plants smell like saltwater, alkali and possibilities.

But neither the rush of the ocean nor the patience of mountains quite held me, so I hit the trail and ended up in Alaska, where nothing really holds. Here the earth and sky do ferocious commerce, and those of us who hunker down between them are always giving up something. It pays to live in a place that works the way you feel inside, and in Alaska these mountains and the ocean, the two forces I grew up to respect the most, are always stealing from one another—silt and minerals, in exchange for the fish. They've forged a tumultuous détente, and we live on the edge of it.

"You are what you eat," people like to say, but I think "You are *where* you eat" rings truer, and maybe nowhere so true as in Alaska, where you can still buy wild meat in the grocery store, and where hunting for food is regulated separately from sport. It's a subtle difference, but a big one.

Here, eating the meat of the land is more than a lifestyle, it's survival. Old John Ireland, a lone trapper and leather worker on Murder Lake, once told me he ate bear jerky for three weeks before bear season in the fall. "That's the thing about hunting something that's hunting you back," he told me. "You never want to smell like you've been fattened up on salmon."

Old John always said he could smell a person fed on store-meat all the way across the lake. After I spent a winter in the Talkeetna Mountains eating ptarmigan and moose meat and potatoes I slept on to keep them thawed, I guess I could too. Wild meat tastes musky and uncompromising, and people who eat it smell wild and muscular, like upturned soil. It's true that after you live in the woods for a year, city people begin to smell like sweat and adrenaline. The first time I tasted bear meat I grimaced at the dank, dark flavor in the back of my throat. But when I finished gnawing the fibrous chop I felt like I could walk for miles. To this day, Montana beef makes me feel strong and rooted. Bear meat makes me want to hit the road.

Fish, though—fish are another thing entirely. A silver salmon that hits your fly line like a streak of lightning tastes the way you'd imagine light would taste—velvety and dissoluble. Halibut tastes clean and symmetrical, and goes down easy. Black cod sits on your tongue like an exotic foreign language, and yelloweye rockfish, which live to be forty and should be respected, tastes clear and wise but if you're not careful it'll make you order too much wine.

You have to taste a place before you can really live there, and Alaska is a land of many flavors—the peppery kick of reindeer sausage, the long-distance muscle of fatless caribou. Salmon jerky, cod cheeks, herring eggs on kelp—the flavors of tides and seasonal cycles, the goulash of life. I have tasted and spat out bitter bearberries so I could hike through hunting season with the flavor of death on my tongue. Once, trolling in Yakobi Strait, skipper Roman Motyka and I cut up a king salmon and cooked the herring we found in its stomach; a good lunch both times.

Some of the best hunting is done at local Alaskan meat shops, where you can buy reindeer sausage made by an apprentice of one of Europe's greatest wurstmachers, or sides of beef raised in the Matanuska Valley, Alaska's Iowa of the north. Reindeer is the only wild meat that's legal to sell, and the local shops buy theirs from Native reindeer herders on Nunivak or St. Lawrence Islands. Some of them have slaughterhouses out there on the tundra, but some do their own slaughtering on the ice. One Anchorage meat distributor hauls the state inspector out to St. Lawrence Island every year for the harvest—he slaughters his own meat where it drops.

You'd expect that meat to taste different than meat bled and sanitized on a concrete kill floor, and it does. They say the human tongue can detect only four kinds of flavor: bitter, sour, sweet, and salty, and every flavor from cough syrup to cabernet is a combination of those four. Taste some Nunivak caribou meat, though, and you'll hold a driving north wind in your mouth. Seal meat absorbs the tongue like a myth absorbs the imagination. It's an overwhelming flavor, and for good reason. You don't go tromping into someone else's mystery without consequences.

When I was a kid in Montana, there were ranchers who could taste a steak and tell what ranch it came from, what kind of feed it had been raised on, and what brand of tobacco the ranch hands favored. Those days are probably gone now, given way to mass marketing and quality control, which thrive on consistency. Today when we bite into a T-bone we don't want to taste the land it came from; we only want to taste our idea of what a steak should taste like.

Here in Alaska, I can't say I can taste those things either— I can't tell which draw a moose is from by the flavor of its flank meat. You can tell the season a bear was shot because bear fed on salmon tastes fishier than berry-fed bear, but I can't tell where it came from. And even though salmon navigate thousands of miles from the open ocean all the way to their home streams by smell, they all smell alike to me. But in tasting meat that has a range, in eating salmon that does reflect a migratory pattern (though perhaps too subtle for me), we feed on something greater than ourselves. Even if we can't be a part of the food chain, and probably wouldn't want to, we can taste the memory of it. And that's something, too.

"Tell me what you do with the food you eat, and I'll tell you who you are," said Nikos Kazantzakis's Zorba. "Some turn their food into fat and manure, some into work and good humor and others, I'm told, into God." Most of us have learned to think about food in calories and fat grams, and where's the God in that? If I were a dinner, how would I taste? Like tree bark and ammonia and pork cutlet? Like salt salmon and unconjugated verbs and Chopin and creamed coffee? My sister, the gardener, would taste like black earth and dried root and zucchini blossoms stuffed with cream cheese, lightly toasted.

Once, when I was young and my family was camping in Yosemite, I breathed deep through my open mouth and swallowed a bug. I became very concerned. "What would happen to a person if they swallowed a bug," I asked my oldest brother, Steve, who knew everything. "They would probably die," he said gravely. For the rest of the day I went around preparing to die, and thought I'd not confess why because it might take the nobility out of it. "This is what it feels like to be on the edge of living," I said to myself, in the way that kids accept the large and small from life with equal measures of amazement and nonchalance.

For a long time, I had a thing about camping with my mouth open. I was cured of it a few years ago when my husband and I camped at Deadman's Lake in the Yukon Territory, the most mosquito-infested place on earth. The dog was so covered with mosquitoes she was a breathing bug hill. We raced like PCP trippers from car to tent, gesticulating wildly, slapping ourselves with dishtowels and camping implements to keep the bugs from sucking us dry. You can bet I kept my mouth shut, real shut, because no emotional scar in the world cuts as deep as swallowing a bug at a young age.

Suddenly, horribly, I felt the urge to sneeze. As I turned my head and drew that deep breath a mosquito flew right up my nose. I sneezed that bug out so hard he was probably looking around for where to pay. After that I thought, what the hell?

And have gone about ever since with mouth and nose wide open, and eyes and ears and pores, too, for the most part. You have to taste life, breathe it all in, suck it right down, until you do die from it.

Zorba the Greek tells us he isn't one of the worst kind, nor yet one of the best, but is somewhere in between the two. "What I eat, I turn into work and good humor. That's not too bad after all!" he says. And he is right. Up here, a licked finger stuck out in the wind might harvest a coat of hoarfrost or saltwater, or an errant cottonwood seed—the implications of inextinguishable life. Every day, we eat our way through a miracle, we roll worlds around on our tongues, we chew up and swallow the Word of God. What we lay down at the end of our daily meal—fat, manure, good humor or something more luminous—depends on us alone.

Krys Holmes

THE GOD THAT WRITES WITHIN ME

The god that writes within me
   defaces walls
     leaves scraps between my breastplate and the spine.
Graffiti whorls the red walls
above the heads of my heart's mumbling homeless.

Some days come on like cougars at feed
and some take you from behind and some
   lay out flat and just go by
and those are the ones that age you.
Never let them catch you not writing, you told me,
feed the days no matter what kind they are
they'll take sweat or blood or both.

Feed the days a morsel, part of a hand,
   your hopes.
Write yourself a new hand
and throw that one to the snapping jaws.
Cut out an eye and navigate
by poetry instead.
   I leap the wild fences
     throwing meat to the galloping days
     —the god that writes within me
     scribbling like mad.

Ann Fox Chandonnet

THE POEM IS SEEING THINGS ALOUD

The poem is seeing things aloud:
the slate outcropping
stacked like lead leaves in a dense folio;
pert rose hips, blood red amphorae
fluttering against a yellow sky;
dark stormfront creeping over peaks
from one welter of water to another.

Each word, becomes the thing itself;
THUNDER,
HAIL CHASING DOGS INDOORS,
HORIZONTAL LIGHTNING
    SILHOUETTING SUSITNA.
Each word sniffs the caraway and onion
in the fat rye loaves
humming in the oven.

Read that aloud.
Let each syllable drip from ecstatic lips
like a bead in a string,
a string of warm amber beads,
syllables flinging themselves into the void
from fingertips like the sign for birds;
big birds; agitated birds,
screams the signer,
each sweet, desperate chirp
a smokey drop
of buckwheat honey.

Marvin Hugo Fuhs

THE VINEYARD

The vineyards that I daily reap,
where each day the crop provides,
I pick from the alleys,
from garbage cans overflowing,
aluminum cans growing in abundance.
I crush them like grapes
placing them reverently
in my soiled duffel bag,
carrying them across my back,
to a place where they and I
become recycled.
Where the wine flows
from an emptied duffel bag.

Robbo

JUST ANOTHER STATION IN LIFE

sitting in union station w/my backpack,
my orange & vodka, my cigarette &
my lack of sleep . . .
a hundred feet above me is
a skylight the size of a
basketball court . . .
it is raining like a crazy
man, it is thundering &
lightning like the gods are
throwing-up upon us from 30,000
miles away . . .
the skylight flashes as the
fluorescent tubes of heaven burn-out,
come-back to life, stutter; while
troops of elephants & rhinoceroses
fall from the sky . . .
if i wasn't so tired & deadened
i'd be running screaming . . .
the man who is sitting across from
me is a murderer the old lady on
the bench next to me reading the
detroit news is

a prostitute
the two cops, one white, one black
both lovers of charles atlas and may-
be each other are walking my way to
arrest and beat me, and that little
girl, the cute three yr old who
laughs whenever i wink at her is
gonna tell her fat & tattooed biker
parents, over there in the corner, that
i touched her naughty place . . .
i am screaming in my closed mouth
running in my wooden seat &
waiting for the skylight to open up &
rain a million shivering slivered
crystals of razor-edged glassy bits into
my open mouth & wide-eyed
stare that tells me, yeah, this
sure is a big-ass train station.

and to think i'm gonna get
married in a week.

August 15th, 93
Chicago

Monika C. Thomas

SALINE SALVATION

Confessing last night's
transgression over bitter
coffee. One hand tucks unwashed hair
behind silver earrings. She slouches
in the sticky vinyl booth, wearing
red lipstick and black leather
jacket, with faith in crystalline
gods and distilled angels.
One drag from redemption.

Tim Young

BUS RIDE

I am on the bus late at night
    windows dark.
Winter's cold grips the nape.
    Slices of the great sleepwalk
move past outside.
Things we have made are more alive than
we
    and are plotting.

Old woman gets on at the next stop
    slowly walks past   sits right behind
me.
Smells of the ocean and the wind and
kerosene.
    The bus is a whale
and we slide along for a while in its silent guts.

Then it comes.
    A whispered imperative
    Mouth like a moth
in my ear,
    ticklish,
a stab in the dark,
    "son," she says, "You need to dream or die."

Ten Rich

TOUPEE

. . . And he sits there, like nobody's business
The look on his face is so smug!
Leanin' back in his chair, hands clasped
over his bowl of belly.

Winkin' at the girls and jokin'
with the men
with all the confidence of Errol Flynn.

Smilin' to himself about his secret
thinkin' we don't know
. . . but
       we
              do.

Erik Wilson

TV MAUSOLEUM DREAM

Wait for the sound of the light switching over
I've never seen my dreams
in black and white
carried to the center of the cemetery
closing
eye over fist at the door . . .

Two masks worn for smiling
bright red eyes and shining
through the many-punctured manskin
shark's breath on the shoulder
where the greasy steam runs colder
and the vertical doesn't hold . . .

Winter and a sharp new toy . . .
the lights go on and on
wrapped inside that white noise rolling
eye over the fist
through the door.

Melissa S. Green

SATURN IS HEAVIER IN MY DREAMS

My head's getting squashed again, all low and squat
like I lived on Saturn or someplace like that—
where the planet is heavy, and a woman from Earth
can't lift her head.

My feet drag like they do in my dreams sometimes,
and I don't know why . . . like there's a path
I'm trying to follow but don't know how to walk,
one foot in front of the other.
I'm surprised in the morning when I run to the bus
and my feet fly, knowing how to move.

Saturn is heavier in my dreams than it is in waking.
I used to peer through the telescope at it:
tiny in the sky with ears—that's how Galileo drew it.
It was listening . . . listening to the dark, and glowing.

I want to call it a she.
She feels like a female to me.
I want to call her by some name
other than that of the old
god who ate his children.

In my dreams she has a deep, deep weight,
and every step I take is made of lead.
I try to put the two together—
the silent, listening ears
trying to comprehend the universe;
the roads I have been too weak to follow
cast in Technicolor
against my eyelids on difficult nights.

I am trying to be like her, listening,
stolidly walking her path along the ecliptic.

If I died now I would remain here, a ghost
haunting places I was afraid to leave,
begging the living to release me into
something that might move—
a river, somebody's feet . . .
Saturn in her purposeful wandering.

I'm lost on Saturn, hidden by muddy atmosphere
from my own ears.

Mike Firment

THE DAY I GOT FLOWERS FROM GEORGIA O'KEEFFE

I was in the supermarket when I first saw them. It was just a quick stop to buy a few bland, everyday, maintenance items and I was impatiently sidestepping the cart pushing throngs making their elliptical orbits of the mass-produced, vitamin enriched, aisles of plenty.

And there they were, bound in rigid bunches, a riotous display of yellow, standing their ground against the dull backdrop of dish soap and toilet paper.

Daffodils. Hundreds of them.

As I held them in my winter wounded eyes, I had a mad impulse to buy them all, lay them out and roll around naked in their soft petals. I settled for a carefully selected bunch of five and headed for the checkout stand, hold them up in front of me like a magic wand.

Magic for her. She was coming over tonight.

Separation was the word she used—a trial separation. Separation to me meant: not together, cast adrift, an easing of the bond, solitary confinement, a dress rehearsal for finality. There were no shouting matches, no dishes breaking, no oaths of revenge, just beers and tears and total confusion. Humans seem to have a strong knack for always assuming the worst.

Yet, we were strangely cordial about the whole thing. I moved out cordially, found an apartment cordially, packed up my ragged things cordially, and had long cordial conversations with her on the phone. Nothing was resolved, merely suspended.

As time passed, I had begun to suspect that perhaps she was right. That maybe this was a good thing for both of us. Then I would have 3 A.M. thoughts that tore the heart out of me.

And tonight, she was coming over.

I had made my apartment as comfortable as a castaway's cubicle can be, hanging my prized art prints, arranging my dubious collectibles, dusting, buffing and polishing away the baleful anonymity. The result reminded me of a politician's smile; it looked sincere but you really knew there was nothing behind it.

It was into this setting that I brought the daffodils. Following the instructions on a plastic tab, I cut a half inch off the bottom of the stems, diagonally, placed them with water in a clear glass on the dining room table, and sat down with the flowers between me and a large picture window. Framed in this window was a February-frozen winter landscape, the overwhelming whiteness of the snow broken only by mottled bands of violet-gray shadow. Superimposed on this scene, the daffodils stood like blaring, medieval trumpets, heralding out golden visions of seasons to come, and seemingly snubbing their noses at the soul draining, gray metal, hardness of winter.

As I waited for her to come, I stared at the flowers. They rose from a fertile, dark patch of leaves, the shafts standing straight, proudly flaring toward the swollen pistils crowned with soft, round petals. The length and slimness of the stems only enhanced the sense of the explosive opening at the tips, and while I knew they were still, they seemed to be shooting up and out and beyond the oppressive stillness. A harmonious union of masculine and feminine, fragile starbursts of embryonic essence, umbilically connected to the origins of life.

Poking my finger into the small opening, I softly tickled the protuberance hidden there. The flower quivered and swayed gracefully on its long stem. The slightest touch would make it shiver. This delighted me and I caressed them all until they were dancing to some silent, eternal, celestial rhythm. One by one I stood before them and inhaled their fragrance; a buttery, earthy smell of spice and sunlight. There were all about giving and gave up their delights freely. I sat back and watched, flicking the overhead light on and off, enchanted by the transformation that occurred when infused with light. I thought about how they were born out of the cold earth, waiting for the winter ice to crumble and melt, the right conditions calling them forth.

Then I heard her car in the driveway.

She came in the door and entered my solitude, drawn immediately to the flowers.

"I got them for you," I said.

"They're *so* pretty. Did you know that daffodils are known as the flower of hope?"

I said I didn't know it until recently, maybe about an hour ago.

She buried her nose in the opening, tracing a finger lightly up the stem. This time, along with the flower, I quivered. I don't think she noticed, though.

Her preparations for dinner filled some awkward spots as we got reacquainted to sharing the same space and the meal was pleasant, having a familiar ring to it.

Afterward, we sat by the fire drinking wine, talking about prior relationships and describing the first time either of us had sex. I realized once again how completely unpromising most people's debut is. It also occurred to me that surely this is something we both should have known about each other. I had just never asked.

We talked about a lot, more than we had in a long time, but we stayed safely in the past, unwilling to risk injury on the barbed wire that surrounded the present.

At some point, I laid my head in her lap and she caressed my hair. Then, she was sitting in my lap. I would take some wine, wet my lips with it and kiss her deeply, though I kept my hands away from the ultra-sensitive parts of her anatomy, as I was not sure I still possessed the right password to intimacy. As time passed, tongues probed deeper, fingers trailed a feathery fire and I found myself overcome with a schoolboy kind of lust. The days of prolonged touching and teasing had become foreign to me, along with the accompanying, stimulating, sense of uncertainty. Something opened.

I had a decision to make, and, though I knew it wasn't my decision alone, I felt I was the one who had to bring it up. Looking around the room, I thought again about the daffodils pushing up through the cold, cold earth. I asked . . . she answered.

I scooped her up and carried her off to the bedroom like a cave man. Soon, we were swimming like dolphins through the warm, dark water, down, down, down, down, deep. Deeper than ever before. No pain, no fear, no thought, just an awareness of waves of sensation spreading out from within. Tension dissolving like honey in hot tea. Long, slow, sweet. Swimming deeper and deeper and deeper and deeper, until, finally bursting, a frenzied rush back up to the light. Laying there floating on the warm water. The earth revolving slowly, peacefully. A touch sending me into spasms. In time, the waves gently rocking me to sleep. Sleep.

She left sometime during the night. I woke and felt her absence, but it wasn't as bad as it was before. I still had something to hold.

In the morning when I awoke, I went into the front of the apartment and was amazed that the flowers were still blooming. Somehow, I thought they would wilt during the night.

You see, I'm still a novice with flowers. I'm learning, but there is so much to know. In time, if I'm lucky, if I pay close attention, I believe I will become well acquainted with them. Maybe then, they'll share some of their secrets with me.

It's never too late.

Carefully, after inhaling their essence, I turned them toward the sunlight—these fragile, golden, flowers of hope.

Nathalie B. Nadeau

Costa Rica Was Hard on My Shoes

Costa Rica was hard on my shoes.

I'm home now, leaning against the kitchen counter with my fist propped into one shoe, rubbing Saddle Soap into the dirty leather. I'm creating a lather and the pale green cloth becomes darker, grey—the dust from dry St. Elena roads. I inspect the shoe as I rub in circles, not remembering it to be so creased and kicked around.

Kicks, that's what he called shoes. He sat at the bar watching my approach and I had my cowboy boots on, gussied up for the night wearing jeans that made him look, and he did look; his eyes started at the top and then down to my pointy boots so I could almost feel a breeze, and he said, "Nice kicks."

The shoes have darkened from washing and it worries me that they still look worn and beat. Far away from Costa Rica, in the soft light of Alaska February, I think back over our trip and try to remember exactly when the shoes changed. I imagine walking to Monteverde in the fiery morning heat while beneath the dust cloud which hovered around my ankles, a considerable transformation took place.

In my kitchen, I look at the shoes and wonder if they are mine after all, because now the dust is gone, and the shoes are sitting there, two slouchy mounds. I pick up the flat can of soap and I read the directions. I realize that this process will take some time, and I am ready to wait because I want the shoes to look like I remember them before I left home, and before he did, too.

I'm standing at the open door of the refrigerator staring at a pile of vegetables which are going soft. I am considering soup for dinner but the whole act of looking into the refrigerator in the first place is just something to occupy me while I wait for the shoes to dry. I imagine that it won't be long before they are ready. For now they sit, drying, metamorphosing beneath the oily layer of soap.

I decide that the vegetables will be saved and from the second shelf I remove carrots, celery, onion, and a soft lump of cabbage, leaves hanging like fabric. I try to remember if I have a can of tomatoes before I lay out the cutting board and get my soup pot from the cabinet below me. I have discovered that canned tomatoes really do something to vegetable soup. In the cupboard I see one, enormous, wholesale-sized, and I try to plan how to use the remainder. Before I decided to stay here without him I planned meals a week in advance. Now my life is different. My efforts to plan ahead have resulted in limp vegetables.

The morning came early for me. It came darkly, too, because of winter. He lay soundly, sleeping still because he is never roused, jolted like I am, still intoxicated from the night. He slept like the dead on these mornings after nights of pool and cigarettes and tequila. I drank from the water glass which we inevitably shared with the cat and turned back to him under our quilt, thick as the snow outside. I moved so that he would begin to move, to change his position wishing to fall back into his heavy, dreamless sleep. I knew that if I continued my movements, short smooth turns, touching him a little with my legs and my hands on his arm and side that sloped down, down on him, he would stir and eventually wake and I wanted him to because I had the idea that we should make love.

I'm not doing this right. The soap is dry. I see that the leather is clean, but it's cracked and dull, not shining and I have been rubbing over and over the same area. My arm is tired. I wonder if these shoes are finished, hopeless. I begin to think about where to find some others.

I bought the shoes in Istanbul. I imagine the shop there, where the owner and sales clerks looked at me with disdain. I had found their shoes, far from the busy tourist corridors where the clerks smile and take your arm, and before you know what's happened you're sitting before a heap of kilims and they begin throwing them back like sheets on a bed and the woman you hadn't seen until she thrust a cup of tea in your hands begins to explain why *that* carpet is cherished far beyond the others and why you will get a very special price. And I did by two kilims, not that day but later on before we left for Berlin.

I think about the kilims hanging on the walls. They are mine. I look at the vegetables and know they are mine. My bathroom sink shines and no dust or cobwebs cling to the logs that make up my home. I value the control I have over these things. I have seized power over inanimate objects and it soothes me. I think about tearing down the wallpaper in my kitchen. I have bought an herbal soap to change my smell. I have lost weight.

He didn't look at me when he came into the bathroom to brush his teeth. I stood in the shower, white lather spilled from my palms like an offering. I remembered when we rarely showered alone and if I did, he would sit quietly watching me through the lattice and plants. He would study me as I worked the shampoo into my hair and follow the white streams as they seeped through my fingers, sliding down my neck and spine and buttocks. He had watched me as though I were a gift.

I have left the shoes on the kitchen counter beside the pot which sits simmering on the stove. The smell of garlic has pierced the steamy bathroom air. I look out the window and between the bare alders which circle my cabin stands a young moose. Her lips curl up like fingers as she reaches her tongue around a thin branch. She chews and the sound she makes is startling, like gravel. I watch her until I realize the hot water is nearly gone. I adjust the faucet and turn my back to the spray. Through the lattice and the thin leaves of the hanging spider plant, I look at the mirror and see my form, solitary and unfocused in the steamy blur.

The night before the morning I asked him and he confessed, I sat beside him as he read and knew that my ship was sinking and I began to plan how I would remain afloat. I imagined myself clinging to the doomed luggage and the deck chairs. I imagined that I had some control over my survival.

I stand naked over the soup pot stirring and breathing deeply the flawless aroma which I have created. I wonder if I've accepted the state of things. There was no inexorable rebirth.

I need some new shoes.

Mark Muro

PLAYPEN

another day/another bad smell

20,000 years in sing sing
and I'll never see Paris again

the ashtrays are full
and mommy's on the couch
re-reading the story of oink
or maybe she's dozing
while oprah interviews
another crackheaded transvestite
prefers bondage to bulimia
ex-jesuit multi-level marketeer
with false memories of parental abuse
by non-biological siblings
with skin disorders

not since nestle's quick
has so much milk turned brown

daddy's across town
building a birdhouse
the boy who once feared powertools
now talks about fish
and fights back with a steel tomahawk

little lambs walk upside down
wearing bright lemon peel raincoats
planets of primary color
spin monotonously in place

"a good wind could pick this whole
place up and drop it down on the mall"

yep
that should make life
a little easier

pretty soon the first grade:

there's a valley, and a school
and a steeple sticking through
the membrane that separates
ape from apricot

the myth of scrambled eggs becomes clear

Mark Muro

TIMBUKTU

this is the place of camels and canoes
where the seeds of be-bop
are traded for a missionary's head
and strings of killer bees
are smuggled like gems

here the sun
bruises the earth with its bent breath
making a dark meal
of venusian lips
mocking my mementos
as the final trick cigar
explodes in my pocket

here within a jar of cataract glass
a mummy bleeds dust
mumbling something sulfuric
turning a flock of crow to smoke

here grass eats meat
and dogs fly
chewing the last mouthful of hope
from a human ditch

here a bush doctor
godfather to marshmallow and mud
spits termites into a tourist trap
giving directions to comatose pilgrims
selling poison postcards
and genuine dung figurines

here I am
smoking a rope
packed up high on a camel's hump
with coffee beans, cassettes and myrrh
watching a buzzard
sharpen his beak on a bone
as the air burns gracefully
moving past my face
in a caravan of gnats

and here the projector jams
halfway up river
a square of white
hanging like a sail
on the dark slide of memory

Linda Kay Davis

INVENTORY

Lately I've started liking yellow
and it worries me because I'm opposed to yellow.
Nothing in my closet is remotely yellow.
The lie of it
goes against the yolk of me.
Charming as lemonade, fresh-squeezed,
and hopeful as tiny tomato blossoms,
yellow seeks blue because it desires green.
The yellow dog kills the bushes,
yellow jacket stings the baby.
Ambiguous as a traffic light,
uncertain as Jello, no
yellow is a dead man.
Besides, I don't look good in it.
Color preference
might be viral in origin,
I wonder if I'm coming down with something.

Linda Kay Davis

ANTICIPATING EMILY

So, you're the gleam
in my brother's eye,
a 22-millimeter Milky Way,
a melody of toes and fingers
on the sonar-scope,
you little shrimp.
I shall give you Mozart,
Aretha Franklin, Chuck Berry,
and what a great time we'll have
hearing all the notes
for the first time.
What fun we'll have
remembering how to swim,
you little Aqualung.
I will tell you
all about your dad,
whose hair was red
when he was small.
And I will show you
that whatever happens in life
   (and it will),
there is always Chick Corea,
Handel, and Bach.

Brian Hutton

STILL LIFE

I remember... I remember I wasn't such a young man, even then, not so tired and wispy-haired and soft around the edges as I am now, but softening, and a little crusty on the inside, as I'd seen some things, and already I'd started sprouting ear hairs and nose hairs that weren't so funny as they were at first, and thinning, I was thinning a little bit up top already, and I remember one morning, looking in the mirror, and looking older and tireder than my old man ever had, back when I knew him, day to day like, when I was still just a kid living at home and all of it, most of it, still out there pretty much ahead of me.

I was living down there in New Orleans, back then, in the French Quarter, and working in a musty, old, used book store, and maybe that was part of it, feeling, what seems to me now, so early old, sitting there all day, reading those old books there, siting and reading all day, right there in the bookstore window, most of those books so much older than I was at the time, the pages all browning and yellowing and delicate crisp, not the crisp at all of tender young yellow-green leaves in the springtime, but all grown brown and yellow and autumny like, and delicate brittle crisp, like leaves not long for this world.

Maybe that was part of it, feeling so early old and crusty, kind of brittle, on the inside, I mean, and looking that older-than-my-old-man way in the mirror sometimes, come mornings, though I suspect that had mostly to do with it being the morning after the night before, and the way I'd spent it, as I was drinking back then, like I had nothing to lose, as I'd lost some things already, like young loves and early ambitions and a goodly part, I remember, sometimes it feeling like all, of my innocence.

There was a bit of a sadness about me back then, I remember, and a longing that I seem to have lost track of, over the years, for things lost, like my innocence, like in some first season of sadness, winter coming, and I didn't know, quite yet, how things come back around again, come spring, and I don't mean to paint it so bleak, though there was that, but even so, it was a great time in a lot of ways, and a great little neighborhood, so convenient, almost effortless, breeze-easy in its way, with a little coffee shop down on the corner, and a noisy little dive bar across the street, and the food, great food, and the music, of course, it was New Orleans, remember, and friends, so many friends and flavors and rhythms I carry a fondness with me for, even to this day.

And even the sadness, well... there was a wealth about that, even, a texture and a richness and a beauty about it, the sadness, and me, just beginning to write a little bit around that time, and living in a city so alive with all and every of human drama, walking, talking, welling up all around me, just out there in the sweaty streets and in the all night bars and in the lazy little sidewalk cafes and coffee shops, like the one down there on the corner, and me, when I wasn't reading in the bookstore window, or drinking, smoking, talking, laughing noisy with my friends in some little dive bar or another, likely I'd be off somewhere, for hours, sipping coffee, watching, writing, savoring the wealth of it, the poignant beauty of it all, the city sadness, and my own.

I don't know what it was about that day, that particular day, or that particular moment, that had me looking up from the book I was reading, right there in the book store window, and over across the street to the window of the dingy little hovel of an apartment, just above the noisy little dive bar, that claustrophobic little dust bin of an apartment, where, in all the time I lived there in New Orleans, as far back as I could remember, no one ever lived, save a series of so-in-love young innocents, without a pot to piss in, as who else could, above that noisy little dive of a bar, all night noisy, and every night, save so-in-love young penniless innocents, so young in love and penniless, it wouldn't matter, and even then, with them, they would never really live there for very long.

That was when I saw her, looking up from my reading.

I'd seen her before, strolling around the Quarter with her boyfriend, maybe gazing dreamy at something nice they could never afford, not now, in some swanky shop window, or carting back some battered piece of furniture found, a ratty mattress, maybe, or some makeshift mess of what might be a desk or a table or a bookcase, back home to their home sweet home of a hovel, maybe holding hands or making eyes, just walking, and the two of them together, beautiful, both of them, beautiful in their way, sweet, and innocent of the sadness, all of it ahead of them, all of it an adventure yet, though I know, I know now, I knew nothing of their sadnesses already seen, still, still and all, you understand, there was an innocence about them, a relative innocence, innocence so close a relative of youth, and still, still and all, me, seeing what I saw of them at the time, and all of what I saw, the two of them, the look of them, the love of them, so lost to me, remembering, longing still, I just had to look away at times.

But that day, for some reason, I didn't look away, I couldn't, didn't want to, something about her that day, something about the fresh-faced, dawning beauty of her, and the way it touched me, just as pure and clean a beauty as I've ever seen, before or since.

She was up there, up there in the window, framed by the faded, off-color outline of the window frame, paint chipped and peeling, rusty-bricked wall face surrounding, cracked and crumbling, the building older than the books I sold, older than the old I felt, behind her in the window, nothing but the dusky dim of late afternoon shadows, sunlight falling full upon her, leaning, leaning forward on the window sill, leaning out and into the light, the scene, the setting, the sunlight, old as New Orleans, Paris, Rome, older . . . timeless, young woman leaning timeless out into the sunlight, timeless . . .

She was wearing a black kimono that day, the jet of it, the soft, flowing bulk of it, setting off her pale, slender beauty, the soft golden fall of her hair swaying subtle with her every movement, she, leaning forward into sunlight, gazing off into the down the street distance, innocent of my gaze, innocent of my sadness staring, innocent of my awareness of her beauty, and how it somehow touched me.

She was eating an apple that day in the window, leaning into the light, gazing off absently into the wideness of the world, the red of it so apple-red, all of red, against the black flowing folds of her kimono, the red of it so fresh and clean and pure apple-red, new apple-red, against the blackness, so all of every apple, I could taste some essential innocence of apple in her tastings, I could hear some essential fresh and crisp of a new world's wideness in its crunch and savor.

Maybe that was what it was that saved me, or began to, the timelessness of her youthful beauty, the beauty of the scene, the black and red and pale golden beauty of it, leaning into the light, all of it, slicing through the crusted-over sadness of my self, reaching deep down deep into some core of me, touching something in me, remembered and real, and timeless, timeless as my own innocence lingering, lingering long past loss and sadness.

Maybe that was what it was that saved me, her beauty, and knowing, seeing her there, that I could love her, knowing I could be in love with her, or someone like her, someone, again, like before, just as all out and innocent as it ever had been, knowing, like something opening up again inside me, peeking out, like some young and tender yellow-green first budding of a new season, some whispering hint of a new spring coming, and me knowing, or some beginning of me knowing, that it could come again.

And it would.

Francis Broderick

—THE UNCERTAINTY PRINCIPLE—

(He watches the young woman step out of her dress, watches her reach round to her back, her shoulder blades suddenly rising sharp and shadowed in the waning light, and unhook her brassiere.)

Woman: Last night I slept with someone whom I had been interested in for over a year. He is a painter, famous in a small circle of painters. He gave me one of the nudes he had done of me during that short time I was modeling. The painting is black and white, two-dimensional, as if I had been pressed flat onto the canvas. This man had never showed any interest in me sexually, even when I was laying naked in front of him for hours. Last night I invited him here on the pretext that a rich friend had seen the nude and was interested in buying some of the painter's work. The three of us would have drinks and talk. Of course, I have no rich friends. None, except for you.

Before the painter arrived, I took his painting from the closet and hung it there on the wall, above my bed. I dyed my hair black—the glossy black of policemen's shoes. I painted my face and arms kabuki white. I wore a tight black dress, black stockings, black heels. I tried to lift the image this man had made of me off the canvas. I made myself unreal for him.

(Naked, the woman takes a brush from the night stand and begins to stroke her long, blonde hair. She looks at the man sitting on the edge of her bed. He is thirty-five years older than she, but still fit, his decay carefully monitored and controlled. He wears a grey suit and red tie with a small, tight knot.)

Woman: the painter was here only five minutes before we made love . . . in the hallway, on all fours, my face pressed against the floor. You can still see the smear of white makeup there on the boards. As soon as he left, I took his painting back down.

I can't stand to look at it.

(The man pushes himself off the bed. He goes to the window and

tugs the curtain back. Five stories down, an ambulance races up the dark street, its wail an almost tangible thing, a swelling bubble of sound that would explode if touched.)

Man: I thought we were only to see each other. I thought we had an understanding.

Woman: That's true, you thought we had an understanding.

Man: Next week, I want you to paint your face and arms black. Next week, I want you to dye your hair white. I want you to . . .

Woman: . . . wear a white dress, white heels. When you look at me, you want to see the inverse of what the painter saw, a photographic negative.

Man: And five minutes after I step in the door . . .

Woman: . . . I'll be down on my hands and knees.

* * *

Man: I was restless, so I had the taxi drop me off at midtown and I walked here. I hadn't gone far when I smelled something acrid in the air, something I was sure I had never experienced before but which was still unpleasantly familiar.

I looked up and saw thin, black smoke slipping out the chimney of a funeral parlor. I went inside and asked who it was they were burning. They wouldn't tell me. I demanded to know, but they were adamant in their refusal. I went back outside and followed an alleyway to the rear of the building where a man wearing a stained white apron stood beside an open door. I offered him ten dollars for the name of the person I had seen slipping so quietly out the chimney, the person whose smoke I had inhaled. He told me it was a prisoner they had cremated, a man who had had his throat cut in jail. His crime had been so terrible even the other prisoners were sickened and they had killed him. The man said that all the dead prisoners who weren't claimed by relatives were brought to this parlor to be burned.

It was one of his jobs to rake their ashes from the ovens.

(The man coughs. He raises a hand and massages the back of his neck.)

Even now, I can still taste the smoke in my throat. I feel violated . . . as if that criminal touched me in some horrible

intimate way. Can you understand this?
(She looks away and shrugs.)
Woman: How many men do you think have left a bitter taste in my mouth?

* * *

Woman: My mother sent me a clipping from her newspaper. Whenever she reads something bad that has happened in the city, she cuts it out and sends it to me. Never a note with the clipping, nothing. My mother lives in the country, in a small house on a lonely road. Last year she fell and broke her hip. She lay on the living room floor for two days before she was found. She tried to make me feel guilty for moving so far from her. She wanted me to believe it was somehow my fault what had happened.

The clipping was about a man who stabbed his young son twenty-seven times. I don't know why I remember the exact number, but I do. The man stabbed his son, then tucked him back into bed.

There was a black and white photograph accompanying the article. It showed the man and boy sitting in a chair, the boy twisted in his father's grasp, the boy's small fingers caught in his father's hair.

They were both laughing in the photograph . . . or maybe they were screaming? I couldn't tell which.

(The woman kneels on the bed, then stretches out on her back. Her blatant nakedness is at once an open hand, a closed fist, an invitation and a rebuke. . .)

I wonder who counts all the stab wounds. If they mark slashes in a notebook as if keeping score at a game of cards.

Man: ?

* * *

(He pulls off his jacket. He unhitches his tie, then unbuttons his shirt. The woman watches him lay his cufflinks, his watch, his succinct black wallet on the dresser.)

Man: Twice, my wife has made half-hearted attempts at

suicide, once with pills, the second time with a razor. For a while, the faint white scars across her wrists seemed to mollify her . . . tangible proof that she had done her best. But I know she will try again. Her own mother had killed herself. My wife took the suicide as a dare. It was as if her mother had said to her: "You're sick of your own life, but you don't have the courage to take things into your own hands the way I have done."

Sometimes when I'm with you, when we are making love, I see my wife drawing the razor across her wrists for the final time.

If my wife does kill herself, I should be there.

* * *

(Suddenly, she sits up on the bed.)
Woman: This is how I feel about my own mother.

I read of an experiment in which doctors removed the pancreas from a pregnant dog. The bitch lived off the insulin produced by the fetuses already formed in her womb . . .

Man: . . . but once she gave birth . . .
Woman: . . . she died.

* * *

(The man drops his pants. His chest is still hard-muscled, but his buttocks are flat, meatless, his legs the knobbed brittle legs of the aged. The woman sits on the edge of the bed. She spits into the palm of her hand. She takes the man's penis and strokes him erect, then pulls him down onto the bed.

She sits astride the man, digs her heels hard and rhythmically into his side.)

Woman: Summers when I was a young girl, I worked at a riding school. It was a poor school. The horses were old and worn out, the instructors illiterate hill people who loved neither animals or children.

Alone one morning, I watched a horse who had broken free of its stall hobble across a field. I stood on the fence, hypnotized, unable to move or call out as the horse stumbled towards me, a splintered bone jutting from its injured leg sharp as a knife.

For weeks after, this horse walked my dreams.

I would saddle it.

I would rise up onto its back, goad it stumbling around the field, always with my eyes on the clean white bone moving in and out its leg. Soon, I would grow tired of its shambling walk, and suddenly angry, kick the horse into a hard, jagged gallop that shook me awake.

I would find myself in the darkness then, in the bed my mother and I shared, a strange wetness between my legs as if I had somehow wept tears there for the awful thing I had done in my sleep.

It was the owner's red-headed boy, a boy who had exposed his erect penis to me, that shot the horse later that day it had broken its leg.

* * *

(He steps from the bathroom with a towel around his waist, his hair wet and slicked back. He checks his things on the dresser, touching his watch and cufflinks. He opens his wallet and counts, then recounts, the money and credit cards inside.)

Man: On the way to work yesterday, I walked by Cooper Square. On the sidewalk were neatly arranged all the things that had ever been stolen from me, things that I suddenly remembered which had been taken from me in my youth. I looked at the sellers—dirty men wrapped in the carapaces of their heavy coats, and wondered what powers they had to do this. Some of the things they had stolen from me you couldn't hold in your hand, you couldn't really even see, but there they were on display.

Woman: Where do you come up with this bullshit?

Man: Next week while I shower, I want you to take four, one-hundred dollar bills from my wallet instead of the three we agreed upon. I want you to fold the remaining bills in such a way that I won't see what you have done. I want you to take my credit cards, the ones in the back, the ones I won't notice immediately and the moment I close the door behind me when I leave . . .

Woman: . . . I'll laugh at the stupid, old ass.

* * *

Man: "All passions are deceptive, for they conceal themselves as much as possible from others and from themselves as well. No vice exists which does not pretend to be more or less like some virtue." Do you know who said that?

* * *

(She watches him dress—in silk shirt and tie, in hard creased trousers that break over obsidian black shoes. She sees the flash of diamond cufflinks beneath his suitcoat sleeves, the gold watch and heavy wedding ring; she sees the power in the thread and weave, hears the whisper of silken wealth and knows how easy it is for this man to pull on who he is, while she must strip off her clothes, scrape the meat from her bones to find herself.)
Woman: *(rising from the bed, her hair falling across her pale, upturned breasts)* You have something there.
Man: What?
Woman: On your shirt collar, there *(pointing)*.
A horrible stain.

* * *

Man: "We do not even know if, when animals tear each other to pieces, they do not experience a certain sensual pleasure, so that when the wolf strangles the lamb, one can say equally well, 'he loves lambs' as that 'he hates lambs.'"
Do you know who said that?

* * *

Woman: I want to tell you something. I want to tell you the truth.
Man: !
Woman: If someone dies in this city, a prisoner, an old woman, someone who has no one or no money, their body is taken by boat to an island in the river.

If a mother cannot pay for the burial of her own child, if the child's own grandmother will not help put it decent in the ground, it is taken away on a boat and buried in a pauper's common grave.

This is the truth. No one is burned. There's no fire, no smoky child to inhale—only an island in the dirty river where prisoners, because it is their sentence, bury your love.

Man: *(shrugging on his overcoat)* The physicist Heisenberg stated that nothing can be "truly" measured or observed, that the act of seeing physically changes what is being seen . . .

Woman: . . . so even the truth becomes a lie when it is put into words?

*

J. Yonug

DIVA'S MAILBOX

WD40+ seeking after or
Desire marriage to
Amateur submissive
Older woman's sugar daddy
Tall & short in all the right places

Transsexual, disease-free
Submissive: someone real
Prefer a group of blacks
Race unimportant
Cross-dressers or transvestites

Horny top down to earth
Monogamous hot macho
With healthy sexual appetite
Be my slave
Member of the armed forces a plus

A healthy vegetarian
Pessimist to talk to
Late at night
To have a baby with
All you need is a man

Looking for morning
Afternoon or sensitive
Evening sexual delight
Your place or mine
Great service guaranteed

Want to explore, eat out
A weirdo Californian
In the morning have a lot of fun
During the week work out
With proper toys to provide

Someone who isn't hung
Up your gizzard
Spank a nasty little
Naughty tyke
Taste your chicken

No obese ladies
Kinky sex or pain of any kind
The rolls must go before
We slam the ham
Willing to try whatever

Clean and professional
A dominant, charming
Attractive outgoing
Classy intellect to
Allow me to dominate them

Lots of spanking provided
Lots of guys share passion
Pleasure and big chests
Beautiful women as tall as me
Very well endowed bottom

For good times and spicy
Companionship it would be very
Exciting satisfaction guaranteed
If you love the
Softness and femininity

Of long walks or have
Never been with a woman
In X-rated movies
Try corsetry and discipline
In a discreet and safe

Sexual environment take
Love lessons from a mistress
Physical emotion a must
Guaranteed satisfaction
No fatal attractions

Any age or race, social or mental
Any species of not shy
Amazonian sci-fi triplet
Seeking mate or
Married woman

Aggressive exhibitionist
Voyeur who can
Talk about their
Fantasies let's communicate
No queenie gossip

Would like kinky sex or pain
From discreet mother and daughter
With a great deal of foreplay
Love to do anything once
This is your last chance

Committed redhead christian
Not fem camping buddy mentor
Oral pleasure fun safe sex or
Toilet rendezvous
Other activities?

Would enjoy teaching
A menage a trois
Reciprocation a plus
Newcomers welcome
Just someone to have fun with

Enjoy massages?
Role playing?
Had your toes curled?
The purpose is
No compulsion

Leather orientations welcome
For daytime activity
High heels, nylon, latex
Evening dress or jeans
Maybe more open-minded

Stop window shopping
The ultimate sexual encounter
Special lasting memories
Relieve frustrations
No strings attached

Help her w/her sexual inhibitions
I'm very clean
Not bad looking
Experienced off-shore sailor
To have an affair with

Sexy woman who
Functions perfectly
While we grow young
Laugh cry and dream
Is this you?

Phone tag companion
100% discretion a must
Never been w/a virgin
Not looking for a garage
To park my car in either

Been curious?
Want to try something perverted?
Ready for a grizzly man
Frederick's girl or
Just a wild time

Financially secure and
Self-employed
Sexually frustrated
Living to deserve anything
Less than the best

Lonely heart
Not had sex for
More than three years
Hard-bodied with
Erotic pleasures

As we talk dirty
It will be a very
Pleasurable evening
A hot sensual experience
Myself or others.

Jeff Byles

AN INTERVIEW WITH THE ARTIST

- *Just what the hell is going on here?*

As a writer, I have a certain prerogative to speak with audacity. I am a bold and rakish fellow, my only responsibility being to my own private little sores, which I must salve continually. Nonetheless, I enjoy an opportunity to air my peculiar worries, so that they may plant themselves in the minds of fellow creatures, and thereby infect the whole lot of us. And I revel in a well-posed question. Hasn't it been said that one good question is worth an entire archive full of answers? You can quote me on that, by the way.

- *Fuck you. Is writing, would you say, an art or a craft?*

It seems to be anybody's guess at this point. Taking into account most relevant discourse on the subject, market trends, and the editorial staff of avant-garde literary journals, it appears that you could call writing a craft. The implications of this development are, of course, profound. English departments have been wracked with explosive internecine battles, editors are fleeing for their lives, and the tabloid papers are making a killing with inflammatory stories on the matter, replete with scandalous photos.

- *To the point, please. What do you make of this controversy?*

Central to the debate looms the ominous and foreboding dilemma of status. That is, as a craft, is writing somehow demeaned, debased, or defrauded? Is it less prestigious, but more democratic? These are indeed troubling queries. Traditionally, to be sure, Art, in all its capitalized grandeur, was of the loftiest order. In terms of honor, nobility, and integrity, Art exuded nothing but the most impeccable character. Hemingway would never deign to be dubbed a craftsman. Virginia Woolf was a paradigm of artistry in its most beautiful and tragic senses. Gertrude Stein, an artiste's artiste. Art meant courage, luster, and genius. Art connotated a pledge of the soul to a higher law, an aesthetic, something one could blow one's head off for. Art was nothing if not worth the price of life in this paltry realm. Oh, for the days when people talked of "inspiration;" when by candlelight one could scribble one's heart out with passionate desire, unsullied by the dinge of self-consciousness; when Art was Art and crafts were crafts; when in short everything was for the best and one could at least contrive to get absolutely smashed on the pretense that it was a writer's duty to wrestle that bottle of bourbon to the counter and empty it at all costs.

- *Drunkenness is a tired metaphor. Are you advocating debauchery?*

Well, yes and no. We can get drunk on prose as thoroughly and disastrously as on anything else. The important point to remember is that the champions of moderation most likely lived extraordinarily unhappy lives. You know, equivocal mornings of starched linens and poached eggs; all the refinements of rationality suffused in the tepid air; a day of vigorous intellectual industry stretched on out toward the placid nighttime. Yes, to everything one ascribes a proper place and purpose: the world is one's oyster, and the pearl is there for the taking.

The trouble with writing, mainly, is that thought abrogates action. Think of us all, scribbling furiously, pages and pages of words, volumes, and eventually library annexes, halls of fame, triumphant monuments to writerly fortitude in the face of ever-impending doom. I envision myself engulfed in wave after wave of my own literary excrement, dwarfed by towering diaries and awash in the tumult of hastily-copied memoirs. Ink bottles, such rare antiquities, rid themselves of their contents, casting hues of ochre, magenta, and pewter into the roiling mêlée. I briefly entertain the notion of casting about for some stable bit of refuse, say, an armchair, before languidly allowing the currents of so many syllables to completely engulf me. There is nothing sweeter than to drown in the unabridged extraneousness of one's existence. This is how I define debauchery.

- *Distinguish between debauchery and literary criticism.*

Where the one can be likened to the pleasant embrace of drowning, the other most properly resembles a debilitating disease. On the one hand, you have the sudden comfort of the accidental overdose, the tinge of regret while rigging up the shotgun, and the aftermath of poetic eulogy. By contrast, literary criticism evokes such scenes as death by flagellation and an eternity shared with skeptics, arsonists, and ne'er-do-wells in a writer's hell. Debauchery, you see, offers at least the possibility of redemption, and the knowledge that one has made some sort of sacrifice, however paltry, in the name of a higher good. Debauchery affords those small earthly pleasures, the privations of which so delight critics. One may be broken, hapless, and deluged with self-sentimentality, yet there is some semblance of that lush, dank undergrowth that so nourishes the soul in need.

Though criticism may be, in the final analysis, the last refuge of a scoundrel, I must concede with a heavy sigh that even critics have their own small part to play in this frail world. Whereas the debaucher mainly gropes about for some fine silken luxury that will serve to swaddle the battered soul, the critic delights in the sort of rough-hewn fabrics that redouble the vigors of intellectual pride. Cloaked in cassocks of coarse wool, critics pace ruminatively through their subterranean catacombs, searching exhaustively for ways to improve upon their austerity. One critic I knew, the poor soul, had taken his vows of literary chastity to such extremes that he couldn't bear to lay his eyes upon any text dated later than the seventeenth century. Furthermore, he considered it a lusty thing to seek pleasure in words. He'd allow himself the perfunctory measure of one word per diem, meditating abstractly on this one word in between ghastly rituals of self-flagellation. Eventually, in a kind of ascetic triumph, he imprisoned himself in a dusty alcove at the Trinity College Library in

Dublin, scrutinizing the pages of the Book of Kells for cleverly-veiled erotic imagery.

Given this sort of unflagging devotion to their calling, I cannot help but to feel something like compassion for the critic. Just knowing that in some monastic cell, there is someone bent over their volumes, confronting every twitch and turn of the page with brazen severity, is rather quite satisfying. For debauchers, in any case, criticism induces the rancorous spirit that is needed in order to keep pushing the pen across the page: one writes most eloquently when one is writing out of sheer, indomitable spite.

So yes, there is a kind of symbiosis latent in the relationship of critic and debaucher. There is a certain intimacy among adversaries, an odd comradeship forged in the embers of mutual, albeit begrudged, envy. In one of those paradoxical truths that seem always to send me headlong into misery, the critic would like nothing more than to be a debaucher, free of the torturous guilts of academic valor; the debaucher, conversely, envisions a life spared from the agonizing task of dealing with the self.

- *It has been said of Samuel Beckett's work that "the self is always in flight." Do comment.*

Literature seems to have fallen at the hands of those destined to open up the soul, and to grapple with what resides there. The metaphor of flight strikes me as exceedingly germane to this self-grappling, in that the self is always fleeing, fugitive, and in escape. As soon as you try to appraise, define, or delimit the self, it turns and vanishes. Coming to terms with this fact can be terribly painful. To understand the self is to understand that there is something fundamentally inchoate about our beings, something deeply troubling, imperfectly formed, and always unknown. The delights of certitude, of reliable truths, of a known origin and a detectable end—these are the forbidden fruits of a forgotten land.

Writing is thus, to use the terms of a relevant Biblical passage, nothing but a chasing after wind, a vanity of vanities.

The self is always in flight, and the only certainty that I can embrace without despising myself is the certainty that we are bound to its pursuit. There are no rules, no directives, no hints as to how to live, what to expect, or where to commence our importunate quest. We are all, so to speak, under the gun. We are desperate, under siege, and outflanked. Our armaments consist of dull and tarnished resolves, with which we must parry all manner of reproach. We are chasing after wind, yet it is all that we know. Vanity is at last our only hope; to suppose anything greater for ourselves is impudence, audacity, and artifice.

- *Artifice?*

Yes. There is a kind of courage required to take this position, a courage unnecessary in the realm of artifice. By this I mean that those who disguise themselves, those who evade the issue of the self, have perhaps looked into themselves the least. One may so easily flaunt one's intellectual wealth, those riches gained by pillage and plunder, without possessing that one scrap of knowledge which actually means anything, that is, self-knowledge. We are apt to go chasing after the latest bauble and trinket of the literary establishment, all the while assuring ourselves that we are engaged in the most noble, respected, and acclaimed pursuit imaginable.

Artifice, in this sense, in the sense of blithe unconcern for the more crucial questions, bespeaks a lack of courage. There is, however, a sense in which artifice resides at the very heart of our quest. Writing probably could be described as the highest expression of artifice. Of necessity, we refashion the world through words, using the artifice of language as our medium. We strive mightily to create ourselves anew; out of the empty page we bring to life, consonant by vowel, letter by arduous letter, the rudiments of a writerly insurrection.

If ever I may be chastised for grandiloquence, it is here, sitting in the shadows, dreaming cigars and scotch: Rimbaud take me now, you fiendish shade, walk with me down and ever downward into the deep dusk of Hades; bless me with your sweet breath, the dank odor of autumn leaves, a wash of amber in the vespers, carry me, carry me. And Joyce, old artificer, stand me now and ever in good stead, gently, softly, supple, asunder. If I could count the pints of Guinness raised in your honor, they would spill all down the waters of the Liffey and leave rings of tawny foam upon her banks. To you and the innumerable others who have shown us how, who have found courage, and who have left his life a little more bearable—to you I raise my pen, risk all, stumble in the darkness, fall down, shambled, weeping. It is enough to be cradled in your arms.

- *Is writing then nothing but a pushing over of tombstones?*

We must work with what has been handed down to us. The much-heralded death of the author, a critical tenet for the executors of the postmodern, has made something of a mockery of my reverence for our precursors. Texts are no longer written; they merely formulate themselves as a kind of skeleton key with which to open the doors of their own undoing. This is because a tightly-controlled literary artifact can always be demonstrated to undermine its own fundamental assertions. Authorship has gained a sinister connotation, evoking aged, balding men with jowls who have committed horrendous though occasionally pardonable sins. While this has cleared the way for an intensely liberating attitude toward literature, it has also shepherded in an age of petty theft, of desecration, and of pillory, all of which serve the dictates of the fashion-minded literary arbiters. Whereas a pushing over of tombstones communicates to me a kind of beleaguered attempt to reconcile oneself with human history, and even seems a little endearing, the recent critical trends seem by contrast to be a callous digging up of graves, followed by a guiltless flinging into the air of the remains. There has been, in many ways, a disinternment.

- *You have described life in terms of fighting a losing battle.*

It is one of my most cherished metaphors. The human

capacity for war being essentially infinite, we are all on the losing end. I hear the clatter of artillery being trundled about, the exclamations of misery out of the blue smoke, the corks of champagne bottles popping into the air as those cynical enough and young enough enjoy the last moments before the ultimate deluge. I've been told that champagne drunk in the face of the approaching adversary can be the sweetest pleasure imaginable: the effervescence a foil for one's shattered nerves, bubbles escaping languidly toward the heavens, translucent champagne flutes setting off the stark gunmetal. The crisp, pale yellow nicely compliments the stark saturation of blood.

I suppose that this image captures the spirit of writing as a battle lost before it has begun, of the relentless quest for the self in flight, and of a persistent striving against debility. The clanging of our collective death knell has been answered with a boisterous disregard. We have no interest in winning this battle which merely installs us as generals responsible for the carrying out of subsequent campaigns. There may be future administrators among us, but I for one find most courageous the act of refusing the call to arms: *non serviam*. I will not serve.

• Blake has infamously divined that *"the tigers of wrath are wiser than the horses of instruction."*

This is precisely, I believe, my point. When approached with a certain attitude, a flair for perceiving at once the limitations, boundaries, and laws governing any given system, writing seeks to transgress all such laws. To literarily deconstruct is to unleash Blake's tigers, and train them on the unstated contexts of power in a literary work. That is, the tigers of wrath attack all pretense, all systems of domination and submission, and all attempts by an author to impose any sort of intellectual hegemony over readers. The tigers of wrath know what an author is up to because they are unafraid to interrogate, to trample, to ruin. Blake's tigers are primarily interested in wreaking havoc upon traditional positions of privilege and power. They are here to symbolize the promise of freedom held out to us in the act of writing, if only we are aware enough to take it.

The horses of instruction symbolize the plodding comforts of our writerly conscience. They carry on their backs the weights brought to bear upon us in the forms of students loans, literary marketability, the constraints of specialization forced upon the patrons of higher education, and the plain terror of thinking for oneself. Such burdens task us enormously, and threaten to beat us into the sod, so much compost for the nourishment of the establishment. The horses of instruction are dear, dear beasts, yet their implicit faith in the righteousness of the system makes them perfect candidates for exploitation. They are used up until their tiny knees knock together, brittle bones shrunken and wasted, their fine temperament now atremble with palsy. It is our responsibility to see to it that we stand fast against such abuse.

- *And so, what now?*

That question, dear reader, is yours.